Readers Love ANDREW GREY

Hunks of the Month

"I thought this was a sweet, easy read about two men brought together for a good cause and unexpectedly finding exactly what they've been missing! It's fun and sweet and features a whole lot of kilt wearing!"

—The Geekery Book Reviews

Steal My Heart

"This was everything I could want in a mystery: romance, sex, great characters, and a miscarriage of justice."

—Paranormal Romance Guild

Love at First Swipe

"Such a fun, short read…if you're looking for something to pass a couple of hours that will leave a smile on your face and a little warmth in your heart, this story is definitely for you."

—TTC Books and More

Dedicated to You

"A slow burn, slow build romance that exploded with heat and self discovery, mixed with a couple of extra intrigues and some amazingly descriptive shore excursions."

—MM Romance Reviewed

Only the Brightest Stars

"I really appreciated that everything wasn't magical and perfect right away…it's a story of patience, of kindness and of facing your demons. These two deserve their happy ending."

—Love Bytes Reviews

By ANDREW GREY (cont'd)

CARLISLE DEPUTIES
Fire and Flint • Fire and Granite
Fire and Agate • Fire and Obsidian
Fire and Onyx • Fire and Diamond

CARLISLE FIRE
Through the Flames • Up in Flames

CARLISLE TROOPERS
Fire and Sand • Fire and Glass
Fire and Ermine • Fire and Iron

CHEMISTRY
Organic Chemistry • Biochemistry
Electrochemistry
Chemistry Anthology

COWBOY NOBILITY
The Duke's Cowboy
The Viscount's Rancher

DREAMSPUN DESIRES
The Lone Rancher
Poppy's Secret
The Best Worst Honeymoon Ever

EYES OF LOVE
Eyes Only for Me • Eyes Only for You

FOREVER YOURS
Can't Live Without You
Never Let You Go

GOOD FIGHT
The Good Fight • The Fight Within
The Fight for Identity
Takoda and Horse

HEARTS ENTWINED
Heart Unseen • Heart Unheard
Heart Untouched • Heart Unbroken

HOLIDAY STORIES
Copping a Sweetest Day Feel
Cruise for Christmas
Frosty the Schnauzer • A Lion in Tails
Mariah the Christmas Moose
A Present in Swaddling Clothes
Rudolph the Rescue Jack Russell
Secret Guncle • Simple Gifts
Snowbound in Nowhere
Stardust • Sweet Anticipation
With Amy Lane: Holiday Cheer
Anthology

LAS VEGAS ESCORTS
The Price • The Gift

LOVE MEANS…
Love Means… No Shame
Love Means… Courage
Love Means… No Boundaries
Love Means… Freedom
Love Means … No Fear
Love Means… Healing
Love Means… Family
Love Means… Renewal
Love Means… No Limits
Love Means… Patience
Love Means… Endurance

LOVE'S CHARTER
Setting the Hook • Ebb and Flow

Published by DREAMSPINNER PRESS
www.dreamspinnerpress.com

HELLO GOODBYE
Amore

ANDREW GREY

DREAMSPINNER PRESS

Published by
DREAMSPINNER PRESS

8219 Woodville Hwy #1245
Woodville, FL 32362 USA
www.dreamspinnerpress.com

This is a work of fiction. Names, characters, places, and incidents either are the product of author imagination or are used fictitiously, and any resemblance to actual persons, living or dead, business establishments, events, or locales is entirely coincidental.

Hello Goodbye Amore
© 2025 Andrew Grey

Cover Art
© 2025 L.C. Chase
http://www.lcchase.com
Cover content is for illustrative purposes only and any person depicted on the cover is a model.

Trade Paperback ISBN: 978-1-64108-822-0
Digital ISBN: 978-1-64108-821-3
Trade Paperback published July 2025
v. 1.0

Chapter 1

Two minutes—that was all Chase Anderson had left before the morning meeting when the elevator doors slid open and he strode breathlessly to his office, past the department admin's desk.

Loretta lifted her gaze from her computer and smiled. "Dewey canceled the meeting this morning," she told him gently. "But he wants to see you in his office at eight fifteen."

Breathing heavily, Chase gaped at her and thought about banging his head on her desk, but with the way things were going, he'd end up with a concussion. "Thanks." Chase shook his head as he looked skyward, not daring to slip off his jacket until he reached his office and closed the door. Then he hung up his jacket, sat at his desk, and quickly went through his email. His inbox had been clear when he left last night, so he answered what he needed to and then slipped his jacket back on for his meeting with Dewey. After all, the world would scream to a halt if he showed up without it.

The company had officially gone to an office-casual dress code. But his VP, Dewey van der Veer, had other ideas, and while he never said anything outright, it was made clear—by his attitude and his expensive Italian suits—that he expected everyone who worked for him to continue to dress the way they always had, which meant jacket and tie, even when it was ninety degrees outside. It would be okay if the guy weren't such a complete douchenozzle. Chase had been in his position for barely a year and had already sent out a few inquiries about positions in other departments of Smithson Biomedical, if only to help him keep his sanity.

Chase knocked on the frame of Dewey's door and took a seat when he motioned him in. Dewey was on the phone and building up a head of steam. "I don't really care. You need to bring this in on the cost we talked about and on schedule. We have three teams waiting on it, and you don't get to tell me a week before it's due that you need two more weeks. I'm paying you to deliver."

Chase had heard that sort of talk to suppliers a number of times. It was Dewey's standard reaction to anything that didn't go his way. Dewey was every cliché of a bad boss, right down to his "do what I say, not what I do" mentality. Others who had worked for him for years had told Chase he'd get used to it. Chase wasn't so sure.

With a final threat, Dewey tossed his cell phone on his desk, and it slid to the edge but didn't dare fall to the floor. Then he leaned back in his chair as though he had all the time in the world. Maybe yelling at suppliers gave the guy a thrill. Hell, he looked like he wanted a cigarette. Everything in the office was designed to keep everyone hopping and on their toes while Dewey relaxed and looked like he was ready to put his feet up.

"You've done an amazing job on the design of the adjustable breathing implant, and we got word yesterday that the initial trials were a success and have been approved to move on to large-scale testing in a few months." As usual, Dewey dove right in and actually smiled like this was all his success, his perfect teeth—probably all crowns—actually shining. Not that Chase doubted he was taking credit for whatever he could, whenever he could. That was his usual method of operation. "The biggest stumbling block is the coupler that makes up the center of the design. The requirements for that piece are so exacting, we've had difficulties finding a company to produce them."

Chase wanted to ask how hard Dewey had looked, but he bit his lip instead. "I see." Chase wondered exactly what Dewey was up to. "I made a list of firms that should have been able to meet our specifications."

He nodded. "And you did great, but the FDA approval process tightened the specifications further and ruled most of them out. However, one firm has agreed to supply what we need." Dewey leaned forward, his hands on his desk, and looked at Chase as though he were being attentive. They had gone through this active listening training a year before, and this was Dewey's attempt to comply with that. Instead of appearing engaged and attentive, he looked more like a constipated predator trying to pass his last meal. "We need someone to work with this firm to make sure that they can and will meet our specifications."

Chase knew the list he'd made by heart. "Which firm is it?"

"Glorioso Metallurgy out of Italy."

Of course. It had to be them. That firm had most certainly *not* been on his list for a number of reasons, not least of which was that they were overseas, and he had been told to concentrate on American suppliers. But just the name brought up unpleasant memories that hit Chase right in the gut. Hell, a punch would be more pleasant than the twisting agony of old pain he tried to push back into its box. But he couldn't let any of that show on his face in front of Dewey. It wouldn't be professional, and it wasn't like Dewey gave a damn about the things that had happened to Chase years ago and changed his life forever. No, that man cared about nothing but himself and what affected his image as the perfect supervisor.

"Do you want me to have someone contact them?" Chase asked. He wasn't sure where Dewey was heading.

"No." That gaze of his didn't shift, but he smiled, like everything was so wonderful. "I need you to go to Florence and work with them to make sure they truly can deliver what we need. Oversee quality and production schedules as well as arrange shipping and be the liaison back to the office and staff here. The project is important enough to the company that we thought we should have someone on-site there." He sounded so reasonable, but Chase was praying for the floor beneath him to open up so the earth could swallow him whole. That would be preferable to what Dewey had just proposed.

"But I'm not the project lead. That's Dave." He swallowed. Yes, Chase had done a lot of the design work, but Dave was the lead engineer and the one who had spearheaded this project. Normally he should be the one to take on this role.

"Dave isn't able to go. His daughter and son are in high school, and his wife isn't able to manage it all on her own." Dewey sounded almost sympathetic, which was something Chase had thought impossible. Dewey leaned closer. "You should be able to handle this for us. It will only be for about five months." The tone was the same as if he had asked Chase to get him a can of soda from the machine in the break room.

Chase could just imagine how all this had come about. Dewey would have spoken to Dave first, and between Dave pleading hardship and the fact that he had his lips and nose buried so far up Dewey's ass that when Dewey opened his mouth you half expected to hear Dave's voice, Dave was off the hook. So now Chase was expected to uproot his life and Ricky's.

Chase's insides felt like they had just been put through a wash cycle and tumble dried. Yet none of that could show on his face, not for a second. He already knew that any expression of fear or dissatisfaction would be used against him. "I have a son in school." Just the thought of Ricky being involved in this was enough to make him break out in a cold sweat. Ricky was settled in his school and was a happy child, and that was one of Chase's proudest accomplishments. After all the upheaval in his early years, the last thing he needed was to be uprooted, and the very last thing on earth that Chase wanted was for Ricky to be anywhere near Florence, or the Glorioso family. The thought was enough to make him regret the breakfast he'd eaten with Ricky just an hour ago. But Chase was like a damned duck, calm on the surface while paddling like crazy under the water, even if in this case it got him nowhere. If he wasn't cool, Dewey would pick up on it and then expect an explanation Chase was not willing to give.

"A lot of the time will be in the summer, and Dave's son is going into his senior year." Clearly the family argument would work for Dave, since he was one of Dewey's cronies, but wouldn't fly for Chase.

Chase tried to think of some sort of argument he could use, but came up with nothing—not that bulldozer Dewey gave him a chance to say anything.

"This is something I'm asking you to do for us. In the next year, if this project goes well, there will be directorial positions opening, and I won't forget this." He sat back once again.

And there it was. The big, shining, gold-plated carrot, glinting in the sun, dangling right in front of him. And fuck him six ways from Sunday if it wasn't too much to pass up.

"This is a very important project for the company, and there will be a lot of eyes on it. Upper management will be watching all of us, so this will be an excellent chance for you to show what you can do. If this turns out well, and I have every confidence that it will, then there will be plenty of rewards to go around." He smiled, and all Chase saw was the damned fox again, only this time he knew he was caught… and not in a good way.

Of course Dewey had to extend the carrot of a possible promotion— one that Chase had been hoping for. Before Dewey had moved into his position, James Sweet had been the VP, and he had been grooming Chase for a promotion. James was a good man and had been a great boss who believed in building up and developing his people rather than lording it over them from on high. "Can I think about it?" Chase asked.

"Yes, definitely." That predatory grin told Chase that Dewey already thought he had what he wanted. "Give me an answer tomorrow and let me know."

Dewey's phone rang, and he snatched it up off his desk and answered it as though Chase wasn't there. Using it as a chance to escape, Chase left the huge office to return to his own, letting Dewey talk at someone else for a while.

"How did it go?" Loretta asked as he passed her area. She was always friendly, but Chase was wary of anything he said to her, not knowing if she was one of Dewey's pipelines of information. Loretta had been James's admin before Dewey was promoted, and Chase had always liked her, but with Dewey's management style, he couldn't take any chances.

"Pretty well, I guess," he lied, and got a look over the top of her glasses, just like she'd done in the old days. "I have a decision to make, that's all." He tapped the counter and then returned to his office.

As soon as he closed the door, Chase collapsed into his desk chair, head in his hands, wondering how in the hell he managed to get into these messes. All he wanted to do was make a living so he could provide for Ricky. His mother, Elaine, was Chase's twin sister and his best friend in the whole world. Chase would have done anything for her, and in the end, after her death in an automobile accident, he had stepped in to raise her son—now *his* son, Ricky.

This was not the life he had envisioned. When Elaine first told him of her pregnancy, Chase had pictured himself as the world's best guncle, taking his future niece or nephew to Disney, giving them drum sets, teaching them about good food, and showing them some of the best parts of life. And once he had spoiled them rotten, he could take them home to Mother. It was supposed to have been perfect.

What little Elaine had, she'd left to Ricky for his care, but to Chase, in addition to Ricky, she had left her secrets and their shared hurt. That was something Chase had hoped he would never have to face again. And now it looked like his work and his and Elaine's past were destined to come crashing back into Chase's life. He could only hope that he didn't end up as emotional roadkill.

A knock pulled him out of his thoughts.

"I hear you're going to go to Florence," Dave said as he came in and closed the door. Chase wanted to smack the suppressed smugness off the brown-noser's face. "I want you to know that…." He looked around. "Look, I really appreciate you doing this." He shifted his weight slightly and wrung his hands. Chase wasn't sure if he was even aware he was doing it. "They asked me to go, as I'm sure Dewey told you, and I pled the family." He grew more agitated. "Things at home aren't good right now. My youngest is having a very difficult time, and we are trying to get him the help he needs, but I can't do that if I'm over there or if I take the entire family along with me." He paled and his breathing grew more rapid. This was a side of Dave that Chase had never seen.

"I get it." He understood family difficulties and drama. Elaine had had plenty of that when their very Catholic parents had learned she was expecting a baby, and when she told them that she wasn't going to marry her boyfriend at the time, Rodrigo, their mother had practically started sewing scarlet *A*'s for her clothes. Mom was definitely all about the drama. "Your wife and kids have to come first." Just as Chase would do anything in his power for Ricky.

"Just so you know, I was the one who suggested that they send you instead. You've done good work on this, really solid out-of-the-box thinking, and that's why we've made the progress we have." Dave's praise seemed genuine.

"I haven't agreed to go yet," Chase told him.

Dave sat down in one of the office chairs. "You know that once you say no, they stop asking. I'm aware that by turning this down I've gotten a black mark with Dewey and some others no matter what happens. But I can't be away from my family for all those months. My oldest will be a senior, and pulling him out of school like that…." He shook his head. Chase would almost feel sorry for him if he weren't so sure that the entire time Chase was gone, Dave would be cornering the market for butt polish. "He plays football, and he's very good. Colleges are looking at him, and that would end if I took them away." His leg bounced as he sat, nerves getting the best of him. "You'll be doing the company, me, Dewey, and quite frankly, yourself a favor by going and making this a success."

Chase didn't agree to anything. Fear warred with the chance to give Ricky more of the special things in life. "I really have to think about it," he said. He knew the only thing holding him back was fear over Ricky… and the chance of seeing Antonello again.

Antonello Glorioso had been the third side in a close friendship triangle. Elaine, Antonello, and Chase had been inseparable through four years of college. He and Elaine met Antonello first in freshman English and then chemistry. Since there were an odd number of students in the class, the three of them ended up as lab partners, and their friendship grew from there. The last two years of college, all three of them had shared an apartment. It was like Antonello had joined their twin fraternity, until hormones and God knows what else got in the way. Chase developed feelings for Antonello, with his dark eyes, long wavy hair, and body worth sculpting in stone. Hell, there were times when he thought a breeze would blow up every time Antonello stepped outside, just to fluff that hair.

At one point, Chase thought Antonello might reciprocate those feelings, but Antonello and Elaine had started dating, and the chance was just too great to take. Chase kept his feelings to himself because his sister seemed happy—deliriously so—and Chase didn't want to get in the way. The three of them had talked about starting their own business and moving to a larger place to start building their lives. A makeshift family of sorts. Then, right after graduation, Antonello announced that he was returning to the Glorioso family business in Florence, and that was the last either of them heard from him. Elaine was angry and hurt. Chase had offered to hunt Antonello down and fill his perfect ass full of grapeshot for lying to them and killing their dreams. "He won't be able to sit down for a month at least. I promise."

She had laughed, thanked him, and then hugged him tightly. After that, they never mentioned Antonello again, except in the context of a curse or as an insult. And now it looked like he was being thrust back into his path.

"Don't take too long." Dave leaned forward. "This is a real opportunity, and you know as well as I do that they don't last very long or come around that often. Take it. Spend the summer with your son in one of the world's grandest cities. It won't be all work all the time. You can go to Rome or Venice for a weekend. And if I may offer you some advice, make sure they pay for you being over there. You'll need a house close to the center of town where you'll be working, and to care for your son. If you decide to do it, make sure you get everything you want and get it in writing." Clearly this was a man who knew Dewey well. Chase had thought the same thing, but it was good that Dave agreed.

"School is out in a few weeks," Chase said, and realized that as much as he feared going, he was already thinking he didn't have much choice. And maybe Dave was right—he should make the best of it. Chase was no longer a college student, and just because he would be working with Antonello's family's firm didn't mean he would ever come in contact with any of the family. Hell, maybe he could kick Antonello's butt halfway across the Arno River just for old times' sake. With all that hair, he might even look like a drowned Afghan hound. "I suppose that as long as they are willing to wait until school is out for Ricky…."

Dave nodded slowly. "Just do what's right for you and your son. Five months is a relatively short period of time, and the benefits of this kind of assignment could last much longer than that for you and your family." He stood and opened the door, then stepped out.

Chase sighed and shook his head. All fear and worry about the past aside, the real ordeal was going to be keeping the past where it belonged.

Chapter 2

"YOU WANTED to see me," Antonello said in Italian as he entered his father's office. Even after all these years, it was hard not to stop to look at the intricately frescoed ceiling of the room where deals and intrigues had played out for centuries. The history of his family filled the walls, portraits of everyone from long-distant Ludovico, who had done work for Cosimo de' Medici, to his grandfather looking down on the current generation. Antonello always wondered what they'd do if they knew the real him. Now it was where his father worked when he didn't go in to the factory, and once his father passed, as tradition dictated, Antonello would add his father's picture to these hallowed walls. If tradition had actual weight, it would be a half-ton barbell on his shoulders.

"Sit, sit, sit," Luigi Glorioso said excitedly in English. "I hung up with America. A Smithson Biomedical person, some American name that I forget. They want us to manufacture for them, and they sent someone here to Florence." He seemed so pleased. Antonello's father was a small man, active, thin, and not particularly tall. But he was a huge man in vision, personality, and expectations. After four and a half centuries as Florentine goldsmiths and jewelers with a store on the Ponte Vecchio and other locations throughout the city, as well as Rome and Milan, it had been his father's idea to diversify into boutique metallurgy, creating nonjewelry alloys and specialized products for very specific purposes. They still made absolutely stunningly fine jewelry pieces, but the metallurgy business allowed the family to continue to grow and prosper.

"Papa, we can speak Italian," he said gently. His father was getting up there in years but was every bit as strong and forceful as he always was.

"No. You must get used to English. I want you to work with this man." He got up and prepared them each an Aperol spritz and handed Antonello a glass. "He is their person here, and I want him to know that we take this business very seriously. That means that we will speak English to him." He lifted his glass, and Antonello settled in the chair next to his father. "He arrived at Amerigo Vespucci yesterday, and I make an appointment with him at the Hotel Hermitage in an hour. Okay?"

Antonello nodded, knowing his father's harsh tone was just his use of English and not intentional. But he also knew that even though his father had asked, it wasn't a request.

He checked the time and raised his eyebrows. "This late?" His father didn't meet with people at this time of the day any longer. After his Aperol, he usually went on to a negroni, which traditionally signaled the start of his father's evening.

"Si," he answered. "I want to get this man started, and he has time adjustments. I think later is better for his time, and I want him to work well with us." His father sipped his drink easily, happy as he relaxed toward the end of the day. "Then you take him to eat, get to know him. Build a relationship the Italian way. This arrangement could be very good for us. Yes?"

Antonello nodded and checked the time once again before finishing his drink. "If we are to meet him, then we should leave soon."

His father shook his head. "No, no," he said, switching to Italian. "*You* meet with him and show him a nice evening. You get to know this man and then you bring him to meet me and we will all talk." Leave it to his father to make plans for him without saying anything.

"Si," Antonello agreed, like he had a choice. Tradition and family honor had been drilled into him almost from the time his mamma first directed one of the nannies to change his diapers. He sighed and stifled a groan. This wasn't how he had planned to spend his evening. He had hoped to join some friends at an osteria for dinner, but nothing was definite. "I'll meet with him. Does he know I'm coming?"

"I told him his contact would meet him in the hotel restaurant," his father explained, which meant Antonello needed to go if he was to be on time.

He went upstairs to his suite and closed the door to his room as his phone chimed.

"Ciao, Paolo…."

"Are you coming out tonight?" Paolo asked in Italian, sounding excited.

"Business," Antonello said, switching to English because he knew he needed to get the language in his head and because Paolo loved to "practice." He loved "English" girls, which to him meant just about anyone who spoke English and had blond hair. Paolo definitely had a type. "My father made an appointment for me this evening that I'm going to be late for."

"Blow them up and come out with us," Paolo told him.

"Off, blow them off, and you know I can't," Antonello said with a smile. Sometimes he swore Paolo messed up the sayings on purpose. It never failed to make the ladies he was interested in laugh, and then they fell for his bedroom eyes and rugged, dark looks. "This meeting is important, and I have to go."

"Okay. I go to have all the fun for you. Ciao." Paolo rang off. He really needed to remember to stick to Italian.

Antonello checked that he looked okay before leaving his family home and walking the few blocks through the center of the historic city. The buzz of people as they strolled the cobbled streets, the scent of Florentine beef, pizza, and fresh pasta, all of it so familiar he could close his eyes and still make his way. And yet there had been a time, years ago, when he was in college, that he had thought his happiness was elsewhere. He'd known it then as surely as he knew the famous dome of Santa Maria del Fiore. But that wasn't to be. His family had needed him, and he returned because it had been his duty.

His father had needed help cleaning up Antonello's cousin Lorenzo's mess. Antonello shuddered as he thought of his cousin. Some men, like his father, turned what they touched to gold. Lorenzo's touch turned gold into horse droppings, great big stinking piles of them.

The decision to return home had been a fast and agonizing one, but in the end, he had chosen his family responsibilities over his heart and the life he could have had. Not that his parents would ever have accepted him being in love with an American. His feelings had been so chaotic and twisted back then. Antonello had been so confused, and he'd thought returning to the familiar world he'd always known would help clear things up, but it hadn't. He'd known how he should act, and almost seven years ago he'd done so, because that was what his family would expect. Antonello had loved Elaine, and it had nearly killed him to leave the best friends he'd ever had. But if he were honest with himself, his heart had been set in another direction, and his main regret in life was losing Chase. Not that Chase or anyone had ever known or would ever know about any of it. His father and mother would never accept a finocchio for a son.

Not that any of that mattered now. All of that was in the past, and he pushed those thoughts away. They did him no good. He had made his choice, and that was it. Still, when he was alone, he sometimes wondered what could have been if he had chosen differently.

Antonello arrived at the hotel and went inside. He followed the signs in the lobby to the hotel restaurant, where he spoke softly with the hostess. She led him to a table where a man stood, his mouth hanging open as Antonello approached. It took him a few seconds before he recognized Chase.

"They said they were sending someone to meet with me. I didn't expect you." Chase's gaze grew hard as he sat back down.

Antonello had often wondered what he'd say to his old friend if he saw him again, but he honestly never expected to, and now here he was sitting in this restaurant. Antonello was at a loss for words. He pulled out a chair and sat down so he didn't make a scene. "My father said I was to meet the Smithson Biomedical representative here." God, he hoped there was some mistake and Chase just happened to be in town. But the fates were stone-cold bitches, and there was no way he was going to be that lucky.

"That would be me," Chase said stiffly, his entire posture rigid like he was ready to bolt out of the restaurant at any moment. "Do they usually send the son of the owner to meet with company representatives? Maybe you could be good enough to let my main contact know that I'm here and I'll work with them. That would probably be best." Chase drank some of his water, turning his gaze toward the exit. Then his expression shifted slightly, as though he had made a decision. "Please excuse me." He set his napkin on the table and stood, nearly knocking over the table in the tight space. The water almost ended up in Antonello's lap.

"Chase," Antonello said before he was out of earshot. "Please sit back down." Chase stood in place, looking toward the exit and then at the still-vibrating table before slowly returning. "I am your contact here. My father feels this relationship with your company is important enough that he's asked me to handle things from our end."

Chase drew his lips into a line, tension washing over him. Antonello motioned to the chair, and Chase slowly sat back down. "If that's true, then tell him that he needs to assign someone else. He is the boss, apparently. He can do that." Anger and hurt warred behind the eyes Antonello remembered so well and had seen in his dreams when he was particularly tired and his defenses got low. Chase crossed his arms in front of his chest, and for a second he seemed almost petulant. Antonello suppressed a smile for fear he'd get either the water or the antipasti in his lap.

"I can't do that," Antonello said as a server brought menus and refilled their glasses from the bottle of water on the table before silently leaving then alone once again.

"Why not? Are you afraid he'll be hurt or maybe heartbroken?" Chase hissed just loud enough for him to hear. "Maybe he'll learn just the kind of man his son is." Damn—bald, cold hatred flashed in Chase's eyes, and then it was gone. But what Antonello had seen was chilling, given the fact that he would never have expected the Chase he had known back in college to be capable of such darkness.

"Things were different then," Antonello tried to explain. "There were things I had to do, commitments that I needed to fulfill." Damn, how did he say that leaving had nearly ripped him apart? Not that it mattered after these years. "I know I left quickly, but I had to." The words left an ashen taste in his mouth, but the complex relationships that governed the way his family and the firm they owned ran were something outsiders just didn't understand. "And that was years ago," he added as gently as he could.

"It doesn't matter. You hurt me, and you crushed Elaine's hopes. We thought you were our friend—we'd even made plans to start a business together—and then poof, you're gone." He shook his head. "It took months after you left us high and dry to unravel the business arrangements we'd already made. You didn't even bother to respond when she died."

Antonello gasped, his eyes widening, the world rocking a little around him. "Elaine is gone?" His throat tightened and he reached for his glass, but when he tried to take a drink, he nearly choked on it. "Believe me, I didn't know."

"I sent messages to the email address I had and texted you, but everything went unanswered," Chase said. "I just assumed that you didn't care any longer. After all, you just left with no word, nothing afterwards."

Antonello heaved a huge breath and tried to process what he'd been told. "When did it happen? How? Were you there?"

"She died in November the year after you left. There was something in her brain that had been there since the day she and I were born. The doctors said it could have happened at any time, but it occurred when she was driving home from work." His expression grew hard, and then he lowered his gaze. "As for the accident, I was at work and couldn't be there with her. She died alone by the side of the road before help could reach her." Chase drank some more water, and when he lifted his head once again, the pain was still present in his eyes.

Antonello swallowed hard and tried to process that one of the dearest friends he had ever had was now gone. His biggest regret had been leaving Elaine and Chase. But he'd had little choice in it. To have stayed would have meant turning his back on his family and their future. As much as it had hurt at the time, it had been the only decision he could make. But that didn't change the fact that Elaine was gone and he hadn't been there for her. Nor the fact that Chase seemed to hate him for all of it. Not that what had happened was his fault. But it seemed his leaving had had repercussions beyond what he had ever considered. "And you tried to contact me?"

"Yes, of course I did. But I never got a response. I texted and called, but eventually the number was out of service. The only email address I had was the one you used through the university, but that was closed after you left school. I also sent a letter to an address here in Florence. I knew it would take time to reach you. I never got a response of any type, and after the way you left, I figured you just didn't care."

"Well, I did, and I never got any of it," Antonello said.

Chase shook his head slowly. "Then you have a lousy way of showing it. You knew how to get in touch with us, but you never did. You left town, and presto…." He waved his hands through the air like he was performing an invisible magic trick. "It was like you dropped off the face of the earth. No cards, calls, texts… nothing." Chase straightened the napkin on his lap. "But as you said, that was years ago." He turned when the server approached and placed his order. The food was very traditionally Florentine, and Antonello ordered without looking. He knew what was good.

Antonello needed something to talk about since it seemed Chase was at least going to stay to eat. "How long have you been with Smithson?" That seemed like a safe topic of conversation. Obviously the past was a minefield of epic proportions.

"I was hired three months out of college. They were a medium-sized firm then, and I knew I was taking a chance, but the job offers hadn't rolled in. I jumped at the job and have had the chance to work on some very interesting projects. We've grown a lot in that time, and I've moved up in the ranks." Those eyes Antonello remembered so vividly seemed to take in everything. So inquisitive, with a light shining behind them that Antonello had always found attractive.

Chase had grown into a handsome man. In school he had had puppy-dog looks, like he hadn't quite grown into himself. Now he had filled out and come into his own the way Antonello had always thought he might. The eyes were the same, and so were his lips, but the rest of him… the years had been more than kind—they had blessed him with a handsomeness that Antonello found stunning. "What sort of work have you been doing here?"

"I work with the sales and production departments. It's my job to make sure that we can deliver what we promise on time and at the correct quality. Which is why I was asked to work with you." Among other things. He and Chase had talked about the dynamics of his family years ago, and Antonello didn't want to go into those details now. Chase didn't need to be reminded, and while Italians of his father's generation believed that business was about relationships, they also knew to hold things close and not to divulge too much. After all, business was business.

The food arrived, and Antonello was grateful for a lull in the conversation. Anyway, if he was eating food, he couldn't jam his foot any farther into his mouth. He and Chase had spent many hours with each other, studying, eating, and laughing. They had always been so easy together. That had been part of what drew him to Chase in the first place. Not that he had a right to expect they would just fall back into the same ease, but this was almost painful. And the thing was, he knew it was his fault. He'd not only lied, he'd kept the truth to himself, and that had brought him to where he was now. It was the age-old struggle: duty or his heart. Antonello had chosen duty all those years ago, and now he had to live with it.

"There has to be a way for us to move forward," he finally said once they had finished their salads, with silence hanging over them like a dark cloud. He couldn't go back to his father and tell him that he needed someone else to be the liaison. It was his job. If he backed out, his father would want to know why, and he'd rather eat nails than have to explain. His parents knew he had friends back in college, but they were not aware of his relationship with Elaine or his complicated feelings about Chase, and all those questions were best avoided like the plague.

"Like doing our jobs and putting the rest aside?" Chase set his fork down on his plate, his expression relaxing just enough that some of the Chase he once knew seemed to move to the front.

"Yes. Regardless of how you might feel toward me, we both have work and obligations—mine to my family and yours to your employer—and there's a lot at stake for both of us." The success of this project meant a lot to the company and his father, and regardless of his mistakes in the past and the fact that his private life was pretty much nonexistent due to their expectations, he wanted to make his father happy and proud. On top of that, if Antonello didn't step up and prepare himself to run the business, his cousin Lorenzo certainly would, and hundreds of years of struggle, excellence, and business acumen would never survive his self-centered leadership. Antonello assumed that Chase needed to please his supervisors at Smithson as well. So on some level, they had a common purpose. Maybe they could start there.

Chase seemed to consider this, his expression one Antonello remembered from their late-night study sessions, except this time it was him under scrutiny. Finally he sat back slightly and nodded. "You're right. This needs to be a success so I can have a chance at a promotion, and I'm not going to spend five months of my life fighting with you over things that happened years ago and that neither of us can change. We need to get along at work and be professional. I know I can do that." But his cold look told Antonello that was all the quarter he was going to get. When the server returned, Chase asked for a coffee and finally seemed to relax a bit.

"Good." That was a step forward and one Antonello would have to learn to accept. He had often imagined meeting Chase again and had wondered how each of them would react, and in his wildest musings, he had never pictured a dinner like this. Instead, he'd always pictured them having the chance Antonello wished he'd allowed himself in college if he'd only had the courage to go after what he'd truly wanted. But reality was far crueler than Antonello had ever imagined, and it had been drilled into him his entire life that duty to the family came first. Antonello was still adding up its cost and was starting to think the price would be his soul.

Chapter 3

"YOU HAVE got to be kidding me," Chase's mother said, still filled with indignation on his behalf, and probably her own too. Mom didn't let things go easily, even at six in the morning her time. "They expect me to spend months without seeing my grandson *and* make you work with that man!" She still missed her only daughter on a daily basis and had never gotten over Antonello's silence when she died. If she could get her hands on Antonello, she would probably change him from baritone to soprano with her bare hands. She had treated him like one of her own, and his leaving like he did had shocked her as well. "You should tell those people you work for that this is impossible and make them bring you and little Ricky home." The news that he was going to be in Italy for five months had not gone over well in the least, so this still had her claws out and ready for action.

Chase rolled his eyes, glad she couldn't see him do it. "You know I can't do that. They asked me to do this, and I agreed. I'm not going back on my word." Any more than he would back away from the promises he had made to his twin sister after Ricky was born. She had made him swear on a stack of Bibles and on his mother's life that he would do as she asked and raise Ricky for her.

"Just like your father. His word was always his bond, no matter what." As far as Chase knew, his father had never broken a promise. He hadn't made them often, but when he did, they were important, and he moved heaven and earth to make whatever it was happen. He'd died of a heart attack three years ago, leaving his mother alone and missing him every day.

Chase held the phone in one hand and straightened the bedding with the other, finding Ricky's stuffed lamb in the covers. He set it aside as his mother told him about the latest happenings with the neighbors who had just moved in and the new fence they were putting up between them.

"Sheepy," Ricky said as he looked up from where he sat at the table near the windows overlooking the Arno, coloring pictures in one of his dinosaur books. He slid down and hurried over, grabbed Sheepy McSheeperson, tucked him under his arm, and ran back to the table.

"Do you want to talk to Grammy?" Chase asked, and Ricky raced over, Sheepy forgotten in his haste.

"Ciao Bella," he said energetically into the phone as he took it, and Chase turned away and covered his mouth. When Chase had returned last night after his strained dinner with Antonello, he had found the residence-type-hotel babysitter, Bianca, sitting on the floor with Ricky, apparently in the middle of a lesson in Italian. "I liked the plane. It was fun, and I sleeped too," he said excitedly, barely stopping for breath. "There's a river and even a bridge with stores on it, and Daddy showed me the Pity Palace." Chase smiled at his son's pronunciation of the Pitti Palace just across the Arno as he picked up Ricky's pajamas and his slippers and placed them back into his suitcase, letting the two of them talk. "Okay." Ricky ran over, handed Chase the phone, and ran back to the table. He never walked anywhere if he could help it.

"I take it he's excited." She was still chuckling.

"Yes, and he loved the babysitter from the hotel last night." Chase intended to inquire if she would be willing to work with him privately once they were settled in the small apartment that the company had arranged for them on the outskirts of the old city.

"I kind of gathered that." Her mirth died away, and her tone grew more serious. "About Antonello…."

"Mom," Chase cautioned.

"I need you to hear me out. I know you were friends in college and that he and Elaine were close… and that he left both of you in the lurch. But I don't want you to let those feelings hold you back. You have a job to do, and since you are determined to do this, then do it well, even if you have to work with him. But," she added more loudly, "don't let him play on those feelings to get what he wants. Work with him, but remember that this man isn't your friend, and he wasn't one to either of you in the end. He may be nice, but remember what you're there for and what he did." Sometimes his mother was so sharp it was frightening.

"That's what I intend to do." It was what he and Antonello had agreed to do, and Chase knew that was the right thing, even if he'd spent much of the dinner last night alternating between resentment and hurt.

Plus, the fact that Antonello had grown into a man with stunning eyes and smoldering good looks made it damned hard for Chase to think. On top of that, every now and then he'd get a waft of scent off of him that magnetically drew Chase forward. More than once he'd had to stop himself from trying to get closer. "I'm not at all happy that I'm going to be working with him, but I'll make this work." That was his goal: do a great job and bring this part of the project in on time and without hiccups so he could get the promotion he deserved… maybe one where he didn't have to work for Dewey. God, he'd work 24/7 for a year to make that happen.

"Guncle Daddy, I'm hungry," Ricky said and giggled. Chase's friend Barry had called him that once three years ago, and Ricky had picked up on it. Chase didn't react. He kept hoping it would fade away if he ignored it, but fuck it all if the damned name hadn't stuck around so far. "And you said we'd go to the Ponty thing." He had Sheepy under his arm, standing next to him with those huge eyes and pouty lips, untamable black hair going in all directions.

"Okay. We'll go in a few minutes," he promised. "Mom, I gotta go. I'm taking Ricky out to see a few things. I'll call you in a day or two. Say bye to Grandma," he told Ricky.

"Ciao, bella," Ricky called, and Chase ended the call with his mother's chuckles in his ears.

Chase tossed his phone on the bed and scooped Ricky into his arms, flying his laughing adopted son around the hotel room like an airplane. "You need to get your shoes on and put Sheepy to bed for the day so we can go out and find something to eat. Then we'll look around."

"But the Ponty," Ricky said plaintively, like it was going to disappear any second. He was fascinated by the idea of a bridge with stores on it. Bianca must have pointed out the sights from their room, because he had talked about wanting to see it since before bedtime last night.

"We'll walk over the Ponte Vecchio, and you can see all the shops." Not that there was going to be much that interested Ricky, but that was fine. Curiosity was something to be nurtured and encouraged. "But first someone has to get ready." He flew Ricky onto his feet and put on his own shoes and grabbed light jackets for both of them, and once Ricky was ready, they left the room with his son bouncing as they descended the stairs and left the hotel. Seeing Antonello again had really thrown him, and Chase hadn't slept well, old angst playing out while he slept, but Ricky's excitement and the light of day soothed all those old hurts away… at least for now.

The streets were packed with people, like waves flowing in either direction and past each other. For lunch, Chase headed away from the bridge, knowing the food got less expensive and better the quieter the streets got.

"Daddy, look," Ricky said. The words had become commonplace as there were so many things to see at every turn. He pointed to the top of the cathedral dome, his mouth hanging open. "It's huuuge. Can we go up there?"

"I don't know." Chase had read something about climbing the dome, but he was pretty sure they didn't let six-year-olds do it. "How about we get something to eat? You said you were hungry." Distraction was an amazing tool, and he wasn't above using it. Using the Duomo as a landmark, he circled the square and headed down one of the side streets. As he and Ricky turned the corner, a smartly dressed man strode toward him, eyes on his phone. He bumped into Chase rather hard, and Chase twisted away to try to protect Ricky and keep his balance.

"Scusi," the man said quickly, stumbling over Chase's feet, and then went on his way. Chase turned to see if the man was okay, watching him continue on, then saw him bump into someone else. He thought it strange until the woman he'd collided with began yelling. Chase wasn't sure what language she was using, but he got the idea fast—*thief*! Chase patted his pocket, and his phone was still there. He reached into his other front pocket, and thankfully his thin billfold and money were still there too. Then he picked up Ricky and hurried up to the woman, who was drawing a crowd and a police officer.

"I saw him," Chase said. Thankfully the officer spoke English, and Chase held Ricky's hand as he described the man as best he could.

"Did he steal from you as well?" the officer asked in near-perfect English.

"No. I think he tried, but wasn't successful," Chase explained and described the dress pants and light blue shirt the man was wearing. He also said that he was a little taller than Chase, broader, with old, scuffed shoes. "I turned to protect my son." Chase held Ricky close before answering the rest of the officer's questions, trying not to overreact so he didn't upset Ricky.

"I'm very sorry this happened," he said gently, but with an air of familiarity that told Chase this wasn't the first time he had handled a situation like this. The officer then thanked him for his help before continuing down the relatively quiet street.

"Was that a bad man?" Ricky asked, looking around as though he were going to pop up again any second. His arms were tight around Chase's neck.

"Yes, he was. But he's gone now, and you're safe." He rocked Ricky back and forth as much for his own comfort as his son's. Chase knew he needed to remain calm or Ricky would become more agitated, and the last thing Chase wanted was for him to be afraid in a city that was to be their home for the next five months. "What do you want to eat?"

"Not sketti," Ricky told him, resting his head on Chase's shoulder.

"Pizza?" Chase asked.

Ricky shrugged and went quiet like he was either thinking or had to poop. Sometimes it was hard to tell. "Chicken and french fries," he said. Ricky's comfort food of choice. Chase wasn't sure where to find an American-style place nearby, but he checked his phone and headed one street over. Sure enough, he found a snack bar that had an approximation of what Ricky wanted. At least it was close enough that Ricky ate it, with Chase having a few bites himself.

"Is that bad man out there?" Ricky asked seriously as he offered a french fry to Chase. They weren't bad, and he ate the offered goodie.

"He's gone, and the police are after him, so he isn't going to be around anymore." He forced a smile, even though the incident had set him on edge. They were safe, and nothing had been taken.

Ricky looked up from his food. "What if he tried to steal me?" The fear in Ricky's eyes was real, and all Chase wanted to do was soothe it away.

"Then I'd chase him down all the way back home if I had to until I got you back." He held Ricky's gaze. "I would never, ever let anyone take you away from me. You're my boy, and I will fight anyone who tries to take you away." He smiled as best he could to try to make Ricky feel better, even though a jolt of fear ran through him. After all, Ricky was all he had left of his twin.

"You promise?" Ricky asked, and Chase nodded very seriously.

"I promise, forever and always." And he always kept his word, no matter what, though sometimes promises got hard to keep, especially when there was a secret at the heart of them that could blow his entire world sky-high. Chase turned away and glanced upward, thinking of Elaine and the promises he had made to her in the hospital when Ricky was born. That wasn't the last time she had extracted promises from him. The first was easy: that if anything ever happened to her, he would raise Ricky as his own son. He'd done that and had adopted him four years ago. Heck, Ricky had called him Daddy or Guncle Daddy practically since he learned to talk. The second promise didn't seem that big then, but lately it was becoming more problematic. Nevertheless, he intended to honor it because it was to his twin and dearest friend, and he'd lost a bit of his spirit when she'd died.

"Really?" Ricky asked, and Chase tickled him lightly to peals of laughter that had other patrons turning to smile.

"Yes, really. I will always be there for you, and no one is ever going to take you away." Chase would move heaven and earth before he'd let anyone take his child. Which only made Chase more determined to keep Elaine's secret, no matter what. He squeezed Ricky's shoulders in a gentle hug. "Now, please eat your lunch so we can go see the bridge with the shops on it." And maybe he'd find something interesting that he could send back to his mother. Her birthday was coming up in a few weeks.

"Okay, Daddy," Ricky agreed with a smile. "How many more bites?"

Chase sighed. "Five more of the chicken," he answered. Ricky could eat all the fries he wanted as long as he ate some more protein.

"Then can we go see the bridge?" Ricky asked, eating quickly.

"Yes. But you have to hold my hand the entire time. There will be a lot of people there, and I don't want you to get lost." Just that idea made his heart quicken in fear.

"I will." Ricky took his additional bites and then declared that he was done. Chase ate what was left of the fries and made sure Ricky's hands and face were clean, and then they headed out, walking back through the center of town toward the Arno River, following the flow of people as they made their way to the main shopping district. The crowd got thicker as they approached the Ponte Vecchio, both sides of the street lined with businesses hoping to tempt tourists with their wares.

"Look at the pretty pictures." Ricky pointed at the mosaic images made of pieces of stone. He pulled Chase over to look for a few seconds before something else caught his attention. Chase lifted Ricky into his arms so he could see better and to prevent him from running off. "There's so much." He paused and pointed once more. "What's that?"

"Jewelry, lots of it. There have been stores like that on the bridge for a very long time. Do you want to try to find something for Grandma?" Chase asked as they paused to look into one of the shop windows. Ricky gasped and pointed to a gold necklace decorated with incredibly detailed enameled flowers. "Do you like that one?"

Ricky nodded and smiled. "It's pretty for Grandma. Can we get it?" He practically bounced with excitement. Chase hated to tell him no, but he was sure the piece was a lot more than he could afford. "Pleeeaaaase," he asked in the same way he had asked Santa for a pony at Christmas, complete with innocent eyes and that lower lip thrust forward.

"We can look at it and ask how much it is," Chase said gently. He turned to enter the small shop as Antonello stepped out from behind the counter, where he had been speaking with the salesman. Chase took a step back, hoping he could get out of there before Antonello saw them. His heart raced, and he felt sweat beading around the back of his neck and on his forehead as his gaze shifted from Ricky to Antonello and then back to Ricky, a realization hitting him in the chest like a fist. Chase could barely breathe as his gaze went between the two of them like he was watching a goddamned tennis match. Holy shit on a shingle.

"Chase," Antonello said, and Chase felt him coming up behind. He didn't have to see him; he just knew he was there. He hadn't noticed the name on the sign, but he must have stepped into the Glorioso family store. He should have been paying closer attention.

"Hello, Antonello," he said as levelly as he could with his heart pounding in his ears. Everything went into slow motion as Chase saw the moment Antonello registered that he was holding Ricky.

"Who is this?" Antonello asked. Chase expected the same recognition that had just pummeled the breath out of him to dawn on Antonello at any second. "You didn't tell me you had a son." Antonello simply smiled, and Chase blinked, trying to find his voice, willing his shock to the background so he could function.

"Ricky," he managed to croak out before clearing his throat. "Say hello," he prompted gently, setting his son down.

"Ciao, bella," Ricky said rather enthusiastically with a wide "look how smart I am" grin, while Chase could barely breathe from the knot of fear growing in his throat. At any second he expected realization to dawn and his life to come crashing down around him with no way to stop any of it. Granted, he didn't know for a medical certainty that Ricky was Antonello's son, but seeing the two of them together, the resemblance was impossible to deny.

"Actually, since I'm a man, it would be *ciao, bello*," he said, speaking to Ricky, his eyes shining with amusement before shifting his gaze to Chase. "He's adorable. Are you teaching him Italian?"

"We want that one for Grammy," Ricky announced, bounding to the window display to point at the necklace in question. "Unless it's too 'spensive." He practically vibrated with energy.

Slowly Chase's shock abated as it dawned on him that what he feared most wasn't going to happen, and he managed to force his lungs to work and his head to stop spinning. He exhaled slowly, his heart rate gradually returning to normal as he watched Antonello and the son he didn't know he had speak together for the first time. Chase had promised Elaine many times that he would never see Antonello again. He'd thought it was because of the mess they'd had to deal with to unravel their business plans, but now he knew why. Ricky was Chase's son now, and had been officially since the adoption. He loved him as his own and considered him the child of his heart. But Chase wondered how Antonello could look into the face of a younger version of himself, right down to the dark eyes, jet-black hair that curled wherever it wanted to go, and a smile that could charm the birds out of the trees, and not see it. Chase sure did. Maybe it was true that people only saw what they were looking for.

Chapter 4

"YOU'RE TRYING to find something for your nonna? That's what we call our grandmas in Italy," Antonello asked Ricky, who nodded seriously. "Nonnas are really important here too, and we always treat them right." He watched Chase, whose eyes had filled with tension that Antonello wished he could wipe away. Hell, he had wished for years that things could have been different, and he knew that Chase's reaction was his fault. Antonello realized it was going to take a lot of work to get Chase to trust him on any level, even just professionally.

"Antonello," Chase said softly, "I know everything in here is a lot more than we have the budget for. Ricky was really excited to see the bridge, and…."

He nodded slowly, holding Chase's gaze for a second, just to see his reaction. "It never hurts to look."

"Yeah, Guncle Daddy. We can look, right?"

Antonello stifled a snicker at the name as Ricky again pointed out the piece that had caught his eye. It was gold with hand-enameled purple flowers on flat beads. Antonello lifted the piece out of the window and took it to the counter, where he placed it on one of the black felt pads so Ricky and Chase could see it better. He already knew the price because he knew everything they sold in the store. Most of it came from their own workshops, and the pieces were one of a kind. There was nothing mass-produced in the Glorioso shops.

"Is this the one you wanted?" Antonello asked as Chase lifted Ricky so he could see it better.

"It's really pretty," Ricky said before turning to Chase, who flashed his son a smile, one Antonello hadn't seen in years. "And it's for Nonna."

Antonello grinned at the way Ricky incorporated the Italian and how he had Chase wrapped around his little finger. "Don't worry. If it's what you really want, I'll give you the family price."

In an instant, Antonello was transported back to college and the happiest times of his life. He was far from home, at his college orientation, trying his best to project confidence and hide the fear that he had made the wrong decision and should have gotten his education closer to home. As he'd waited for the day to begin, a pair of twins sat down next to him, speaking so quickly he could barely understand a word they said.

"Are you okay?" Elaine had asked him much more slowly. "You look pale."

Antonello had swallowed hard. "Just wondering if my English is good enough. Maybe I should have gone to school in Bologna. You speak fast, and I didn't understand any of it."

Chase had smiled wide enough to light up his eyes. "Don't pay attention to us. We're twins, and sometimes we slip into a sort of communication shorthand." He pulled out a notebook and set it on the long lecture hall table. "I'm Chase, and this is my sister, Elaine." He held out his hand. Antonello shook it, and in an instant, he'd felt that first spark of attraction, one he knew he had to deny.

"Don't worry," Elaine said with a smile nearly identical to her brother's. "We'll watch out for you." And they had. Within weeks, they became inseparable and as close as, or closer than, family.

"You don't have to do that," Chase said, snapping Antonello out of the past.

"Of course I do," Antonello told him softly. "Freshman biology," he said, leaning slightly over the counter.

Chase's expression softened slightly, some of the wariness leaving his eyes until finally Chase smiled at him, a real smile that turned into laughter that carried Antonello right along with it. Damn, that was good to see, and it gave Antonello hope that they could eventually get along and that maybe Chase wouldn't rip him to pieces if he got the chance.

"What's so funny?" Ricky asked, looking at both of them like they had lost their minds.

"Nothing," Chase told him, still chuckling. "Just Mr. Antonello trying to dissect a fish, but he lost the instructions, and in the end he ended up filleting it like he was going to eat it for dinner."

"Fish are yucky," Ricky pronounced and turned back to the necklace. "Can we get it for Nonna?" The kid had a one-track mind.

"How about if I put it aside for you until you can make a decision?" Antonello offered and pulled out a felt bag. He slipped the piece inside and added Chase's name and a hold note before putting it behind the counter. "Okay?"

"Daddy," Ricky said, that lower lip sticking out.

"I'll think about it," Chase said to Ricky before turning to Antonello with his gaze so intent Antonello could feel him searching for Antonello's motive. But then he held out his hand to Ricky. "Now, we should let Mr. Antonello get back to work. Tell him thank you for helping us."

Ricky waved with a smile. "Thank you." They went through the door, and Antonello couldn't help following them out of the shop, watching as Chase and Ricky continued across the Arno. Once they disappeared from sight, he returned inside.

"Something catch your eye, cousin?" Lorenzo said in Italian from behind him, setting Antonello's teeth on edge in an instant. He turned and forced a smile to throw his cousin off the scent.

"I was just visiting with an old friend." Elaine might have expected him to call Chase a frenemy. He had heard her use that term a few times, and she had explained it to him. Not that Antonello intended to take the time to explain it to his cousin. He wasn't worth the effort.

"She must be really something from the way you watched her." Sometimes his cousin saw too much, but he mustn't have seen Chase and Ricky, which was a relief. "There's plenty to look at today, but none of them compare to Gina here," he added in English, flashing a smile at the beautiful woman with dark Spanish eyes on his arm, and she smiled, leaning a little closer to his smarmy relative. Antonello wanted to tell her to run for the hills, but she seemed besotted.

"Like I haven't heard that line before. Maybe you should get some new material," Antonello said in Italian as he flashed his biggest smile, figuring Gina didn't understand it.

"Look who thinks he's funny," Lorenzo retorted, his lips curling downward just enough for Antonello to notice. He liked that he had gotten under Lorenzo's skin. His uselessness had been demonstrated more than once, including his last foul-up, which had nearly cost the firm a valued customer in Milan. All because Lorenzo had no idea that when the customer specified Au on the order, they were using the chemical symbol for gold. They were a metallurgical company, and they used chemical symbols every day. God knows what Lorenzo thought, but it almost cost the company a lot of money as well as a longtime customer. As usual, Antonello had been called in to repair the damage.

Rather than prolong the conversation, he tried to get to the point. "What are you doing here?" Lorenzo had no real interest in the family business other than what the money it could generate might buy him or using his last name to impress. Beyond that, he couldn't care less.

"I thought I'd see if there was something in the store that Gina might like." He made it sound like he would simply walk in and take what he wanted for some girl who was willing to be seen on his arm. Lorenzo definitely had a type: female, beautiful, and preferably just passing through. He could wine, dine, and get what he wanted from them with no chance of a commitment. The one Antonello felt sorry for was Lorenzo's wife. Lorenzo had no shame at all and loved being seen with pretty women. Antonello was pretty sure that Aria was well aware of how her husband behaved. What he didn't understand was why she put up with it.

Antonello stepped a little closer and lowered his voice, switching to Italian. "Sorry, but not today. You've pulled that trick enough that your account has been closed. You pay full price and in cash." With that message imparted, he figured it was time to deal with the real elephant in the room. "Does Gina know you have a wife who will castrate you if you do anything with this girl?" He kept his voice light, but he wanted Lorenzo to know that he was on very thin ice. His cousin needed to grow up and stop acting like a stupid teenager.

Lorenzo paled and cleared his throat.

Once again Antonello flashed a smile. "Have a good day, cousin. You too, Gina. Enjoy your stay in Florence." Antonello waited until they moved off the Ponte Vecchio before returning inside the shop and made a point of reminding Claudio and Renate, the team who ran the shop for his family, that Lorenzo's days of shopping on the family dime were over. Not that either of them liked Lorenzo anyway, and he was fairly certain that if Antonello wasn't here, Claudio would be more than happy to send Lorenzo on his way.

"Is there anything more that you need, sir?" Renate asked. "Claudio and I can handle things." Renate had been working in the shop for thirty years and probably knew more about it than Antonello ever would. She immediately fussed in the window, replacing the piece Antonello had removed, and like clockwork, two couples came inside, interested in the new piece. Antonello knew that he wasn't needed and thanked both of them before heading away from the river toward the Duomo and the center of the old city.

To his surprise, it was a relatively quiet day. The square outside the cathedral had the usual line of tourists waiting to get inside, along with a separate line to view the baptistry and bell tower.

"But I wanna go up there." That voice caried on the breeze, and Antonello turned to where Chase and Ricky stood in one of the shadows, with Ricky pointing toward the top of the dome. "Can we go?"

"I don't think you're old enough," Chase said as Antonello waved. Ricky waved back and then broke away from his dad and ran up to Antonello. "Do they allow kids up there?"

"Ricky…," Chase scolded as he approached. "I'm sorry. Once he gets something in his mind, he gets pretty stubborn." He rolled his eyes just like he used to in college. "I have no idea where he gets that from." He smiled once more. "He wants to climb the dome, but I think he's probably too young." Chase held out his hand, and Ricky took it, looking up at Antonello like he was some sort of savior and the kid's very last hope. It was adorable.

"You have to have a time slot, and they are very hard to get," Antonello said. "And it's a lot of stairs, like over four hundred."

Ricky's mouth hung open.

"How about we get gelato instead?" Chase was clearly trying to divert the kid.

Antonello decided to play into the redirection. "I know the best place," he offered and then paused, because he had allowed to let himself get excited at the prospect of spending a little more time with Chase, and he hadn't been asked. "It's around the far side of the Duomo and then a block down the street next to the museum. You can't miss it, and they make all their own, so it's really good." He smiled and took a step back. Having Chase here was getting into his head, and he needed to stop that. They had agreed to work together and nothing more. That was all Chase wanted. Not that Antonello could blame him after how he had treated him and his sister after college. "You two have fun." His original intention had been to get himself an afternoon pastry, but he wasn't in the mood any longer.

He checked the time and tried to remember if he had eaten lunch and decided what he truly needed was something a little more substantial than pastry.

"Mr. Nello, Mr. Nello." Ricky ran around people before barreling into him. "You come too."

"Where is…?" Before he could finish his sentence, Chase hurried up.

"Don't run away like that," Chase scolded. "Remember the bad man from earlier?" Ricky's expression immediately grew serious, and he nodded. "Just stay with me."

"But Guncle Daddy, Mr. Nello needs ice cream too. I can tell." He said it with such conviction that Chase seemed to cave in.

"I'm sure you have plenty to do," Chase said softly.

"But he *needs* it," Ricky said.

Chase scooped up the boy, twirling him around to fits of laughter. "Oh, does he really? Or is that your way of saying that *you* want gelato?" Chase ticked Ricky until he squirmed, laughter following more laughter. Chase stopped his tickling and Ricky settled in his arms, his smile huge.

"I want Mr. Nello to come with us," Ricky said, and Antonello nodded and ended up leading the way to the best gelato in Florence.

Ricky looked over the case with his mouth open while Chase tried to help him figure out what he wanted. Antonello got a combination of chocolate and pistachio. "Do you still like mango?" he asked Chase quietly, getting a raised eyebrow in return before Chase ordered exactly that.

"How did you remember that?" Chase asked.

Antonello shrugged to avoid saying that he remembered everything about their time together. Those years were some of the happiest he'd ever had. Chase grabbed some napkins, and once Ricky chose raspberry and chocolate, they sat down at one of the tables outside the door, watching as half the tourist world walked past.

"This is part of what I love about living here," Antonello said as he waved to family friends as they walked arm in arm down the street the way they had every evening for decades. "There's the familiar mixed with the ever-changing. It's like going to the museums here and seeing things that have been around for centuries, and yet a few miles away from the river are galleries featuring new artists with new ways of expressing themselves. It's all right here." He sat back.

"I never thought of it that way." Chase lightly wiped Ricky's fingers with a napkin. Then he set the napkin aside and finished his gelato. "Everything I've seen of the city is so vibrant, but historic and…."

"That may be true. My family has a long history here, and part of what we do is steeped in that, like the necklace that Ricky picked out this afternoon. Those designs have been around for hundreds of years. Some of them date to the time of Lorenzo the Magnificent. But underneath those designs are modern methods for manipulating the metals. And then on top of that we've built a whole new business that fully exists in the modern world, but like everything else rests on the foundations laid hundreds of years ago." He finished his gelato and put the cup in the trash.

"Daddy," Ricky said, pulling their attention.

"Was that good?" Chase asked, and Ricky nodded. Chase wiped his hands again and gave Ricky a clean napkin to wipe his face. "Are you happy?"

Ricky turned, looking around, and then pointed. "Can we go up there now?"

Antonello chuckled as Chase rolled his eyes.

"Not now," Chase said gently. "You and I are going to be here for a while, and there will be plenty of time for us to do everything. Okay?" He shifted Ricky onto his lap as he finished his gelato. Then Chase and Ricky got up, with Ricky holding Chase's hand.

"We should get home. I'm sure you have things you need to do, and I have plenty that I have to do before Monday. We can go through the detailed specifications for the part to make sure everything is exactly as it should be before we begin any sort of production."

In an instant, Antonello was reminded that his relationship with Chase was strictly business. Anything more was foolish, and he needed to keep that in mind. "Have a great rest of the weekend, and I'll see you Monday." Antonello stayed seated as Chase and Ricky walked back toward the Duomo.

"Ciao, bello, Mr. Nello," Ricky cried as he turned around. Antonello waved, and Ricky returned it before continuing away with Chase. It was so easy to get sucked into the past and feelings he should have buried a long time ago. Still, as much as he told himself that he wasn't going to do it, Antonello watched them go, then finally stood to throw away the last of the trash once they had turned the corner and were out of sight. He debated going home, but he headed to the office instead. He had nothing else to do, and if Chase was determined to be uber-prepared, he was damned well going to do the same.

Chapter 5

Chase closed Ricky's bedroom door, breathing a sigh of relief. Sunday had been rainy, so he and Ricky spent most of the day at home. In the afternoon, during a break between storm bands, they had returned to the jewelry store to purchase the necklace. Antonello hadn't been there, much to Chase's relief, but he had kept his promise and made sure they got a very good price. Ricky had been thrilled that he was able to get something special for Grandma, and he practically danced all the way home.

"Is it a surprise?" Ricky asked. "Can I tell her?"

"Let's wait until her birthday, okay?" He put his finger over his lips, and Ricky did the same, though Chase was pretty sure he would spill the beans the next time he talked to Grandma, and that was okay. It was still worth a shot.

Chase returned to the living room and put on a movie and was just settling to watch when his phone rang. He checked the caller ID and answered it. "Hey, Mom," he said softly, pausing the movie. "What's up?" He had debated telling his mother his suspicion that Antonello was Ricky's father, but decided there was no need to upset her, especially since he didn't have a way to prove it, and if he were wrong, then she'd get upset about nothing.

"Are you and Ricky okay? I haven't heard from you, and…." It had only been a day, but his mom was probably still getting used to the idea of them being here.

"Everything is fine here so far. I've met with the people I'm going to work with." Something was bothering her; he could tell by her tone of voice.

"And it's him, isn't it? You're stuck working with him." The vehemence in her voice took Chase off guard, but it probably shouldn't have. "I found some of the photo albums…." Chase stifled a groan. He could just imagine his mother sitting on the sofa looking at pictures of Elaine, getting sadder and angrier by the second. "I hate that man. He hurt her so much, and then she…."

"Are you drinking?" The tinkling of ice in the glass gave it away. His mother loved her whiskey sours, and he wondered how many she'd had before calling.

"Mind your own business."

"I'll take that as a yes." He took a deep breath to steady himself. "This is my job, and I have to be here. And I know you aren't happy that they designated Antonello as their lead on the project."

She grew quiet for a second. "I should come over there and...." Now her words were slurring. That was all Chase needed—a half-drunk call from his mother. He was the one working with Antonello for the next five months, and he knew he could do it, regardless of the old feelings that threatened to reignite every damned time he saw him. Not that it mattered. They would work together and that was all. Period.

"You need to calm down, please. I'm just working with him. It's a professional relationship. I made that very clear up front. So you can stop worrying. And please, put the photo albums away and your glass in the sink." It was only five in the evening there, and she was already sloshed. "Maybe you should lie down for a little while." And sober up— though he kept that part to himself. He didn't need a blow-up the size of a Vesuvius eruption.

"I'm not drunk, I'm...." She sniffled lightly. "You're all gone, and it's going to be months until I see my grandson again." She was drinking again, the ice-on-the-glass sound as clear as a bell.

"He's in bed now, but we'll Facetime you later in the week so the two of you can see each other and talk. I promise."

"He's going to forget me," she said. Mom was passing slightly drunk and was well on her way to maudlin.

"No, he isn't." Chase checked the time. "It's getting late here, and I need to be in the office in the morning and ready to hit the ground running. My boss is going to want a report as soon as he comes into the office at about two Florence time, which gives me just six hours to get together what he's going to want to hear." And of course he was going to expect a week's worth of work in that time because that was the kind of dick boss he was. "We'll call you during the week." He told her goodbye and waited until she hung up before ending the call on his side.

Jesus. He sighed. He was starting to feel like a juggler, balancing his boss, Antonello, his mother, and the largest ball of all, his suspicion that Antonello might be Ricky's father. There was nothing he could do about his boss, other than do his job. His mother—well, she was who she was. And as far as Antonello was concerned, keeping to a strictly professional relationship would kill two birds with one stone. It would make sure those residual feelings stayed in their damned box, and it would keep Ricky and Antonello apart and his suspicions about Ricky's parentage out of mind.

He still couldn't believe Antonello hadn't been able to see how much Ricky looked like the kid version of him, down to the eyes, that damned grin that always managed to get around Chase's defenses, and the same jet-black hair that was always determined to do what it wanted. Though as Chase thought about it, Rodrigo had some of those same qualities, and it was possible he was seeing things that weren't there. He shook his head to stop the thoughts from whirling him into a migraine. Whether Rodrigo or Antonello was Ricky's biological father didn't matter. He was only here for a few months, and then he and Ricky would return home to their real lives. And all he had to do to avoid any of those questions was keep Antonello and Ricky apart, which should be easy as long as he could keep his and Antonello's dealings on a work basis only.

Chase arrived at the Glorioso offices just outside the historic center a few minutes after eight. He hadn't quite known what to expect, but a young woman at the front desk was ready for him. She phoned, and Antonello came down to get him and escorted Chase up to the third floor.

"This building was constructed in the late 1600s, and while the inside has been renovated, it's a bit haphazard yet because it's still historic." He pushed open the door to a small room that had Chase looking upward to molded ceilings with a mural depicting what seemed like motherhood in the center.

"Is this where all the businesses are managed?"

"It is now," Antonello said as he motioned Chase to a wooden desk with a phone. "My father maintains his office in the traditional center of business, where it's been for centuries. This building came up for sale at the same time we were expanding, so he purchased it and set about renovating what was beyond repair and restoring what was worth saving. This small space will be your office, and that door leads to mine. In the original home, this was the nursery."

"Jesus," Chase muttered.

"This home was built by one of my ancestors, so Father was more than a little pleased to have it back in the family." He stood by the door, and Chase wondered what else there was to say. He stayed there until Chase turned, trying not to admire him, which was hard because Antonello had always been stunning, and the man had only improved with time.

"Is there something you needed?" Chase asked, reminding himself to be professional and keep at bay all thoughts of what Antonello might look like without that shirt, no matter what his open collar hinted at. "I thought that if you have time, we could review the specifications this morning and make sure what you have is exactly what we need."

"I have you in at half past nine. I will bring what we are working from." He hesitated before pulling open the door that connected the two offices and going into his own.

Chase shook his head slightly before sitting down and pulling out his laptop. He connected to the internet using the codes that were on the desk and tried to get his mind on the tasks at hand. He was hoping to head off Dewey's annoying questions, so he composed an email of his plans and goals for the week, along with the schedule he anticipated, and sent that to him so it would be there, waiting, when he got into the office. Then he set about preparing for his meeting.

"WHAT IS this?" Chase asked, looking over the papers Antonello had brought with him.

"The exact chemical makeup of the alloy. It matches this portion of the specifications, and we converted it to this exact alloy, which is what you said you wanted. We will then take that and process it into the part. It's going to be more resilient and last longer if we cast the general shape and then mill the part to the exact specs. Any deficiencies that might creep into the casting will show up in the milling. If it can withstand the exacting process, it will more than meet your specs, and it isn't going to add to the cost. It's all done by machine, and the end product is tested before packaging and shipping."

Chase nodded, seeing the benefit of what Antonello was explaining. He compared it to the base specs supplied and prepared to send the information to Dave for his review and approval. "How long will it take to begin production?"

"As soon as we get signoff on the designs, we'll begin preparations and then set up the process. That usually takes about two to three weeks. We'll do some test runs and check them out thoroughly before delivering the first prototypes to you for verification and your testing. After that, it's up to your testing staff, as well as regulatory approval. Once you give the word, we'll ramp up to initial production levels, which will take a few months. Part of how we'll keep costs down is a steady stream of smaller deliveries rather than a huge run with a large single delivery. You'll need to specify the number of units and when they'll be needed." He made it sound so simple, but Chase knew that there were a million and one things that could go wrong; there always were.

"All right. I need to get all this written up and over to the team in the States for their review. My boss is going to need to sign off, and that could take a few days." And a lot of work on his part making and highlighting the updates to the process specified and making sure it was in language Dewey could understand.

"Very good." Antonello leaned back in the chair behind his desk. "I expected there would be some time needed. If you like, go ahead and make your updates. If you want me to review them, I'll be happy to, just to ensure there is no miscommunication."

"All right." Chase wanted to get out of the office and back to his own. Antonello's citrusy cologne mixed with his natural scent was driving Chase crazy and making it difficult for him to concentrate. Once again he reminded himself that any sort of attraction to Antonello came with pitfalls that he had to avoid. "It will take some time for me to get everything together." He hurried out of Antonello's office and sat at his temporary desk just to clear his head.

"ANTONELLO," HE said, bringing his laptop to the next office. Another man sat on the corner of Antonello's desk, looking like he was making himself cozy. Chase cleared his throat, and they both looked at him.

"You must be the American. I am Paolo. It's nice for you to meet me."

Antonello groaned. "You're supposed to say it's nice to meet you."

"I'm sorry. My English, it slides sometimes," Paolo said with an almost seductive smile and sparkling eyes, and Chase wondered if they were for him or for Antonello. "I am glad to meet you." He turned to Antonello. "Right?"

"You speak better English than that, so stop trying to be endearing. It won't work." Antonello stood. "Paolo is a friend."

"I see." Okay, so part of him wanted to gouge Paolo's eyes out. Not that he had a right to that kind of reaction, and it went against the whole being professional thing, but still. Chase could see this guy was a player from a mile—and a language barrier—away. He was not going to push for a further definition of what "friend" meant. Though the guy was sitting on Antonello's desk, making himself very much at home.

"What did you want?" Antonello asked Paolo. "Some of us have work to do, and you draping yourself over my desk isn't helping. Go find yourself someone to occupy you for a few hours."

Paolo put his hands over his heart. "Your arrows wound me." So he was a drama queen to boot. "I came to see if you wanted to go out tonight. There's a big celebration across the Arno, and it's summer. We can pick on all the lovely girls who are… warm?"

Chase wondered if this guy was for real, and it was even more amusing that he was likely straight. "Do women really respond to that kind of routine?" If they did, Chase felt sorry for them. The women he knew were more interested in a guy who was sincere as opposed to acting like some sort of idiom-flubbing clown.

"Hey. I'm cute… no?" He put his hands in the air like his looks made up for everything. "And the women like me." He paused. "Him," he said, looking to Antonello, "I'm not so sure. It's been a long time since he went out and had fun. You work too much and spend all your time with business." In Chase's experience, women had always liked Antonello, and in college there had been plenty of admirers, as well as himself. Not that anything had come of it, even if the two of them had flirted pretty hard more than once. Chase was fairly sure that Antonello was at least bisexual, but he wasn't about to share those suspicions. That was Antonello's business and not his to share.

Antonello switched to Italian, and the two of them had a quick but heated-sounding discussion. Chase wondered if he should return to his office, but Antonello switched back to English. "You go and have fun. I have a commitment already."

Paolo slipped off Antonello's desk with a dramatic sigh. "You are going to end up a male old maid if you are not careful. And I bet I said that right." Chase couldn't help smiling and flashing a thumbs-up. Paolo laughed as he strode out of the office. "Ciao." Chase wouldn't be surprised if he stopped at every desk along the way to talk to each of the ladies as he passed by.

"He and I have been friends since we were children. My father and his father are… like brothers." Antonello sat back down. "There was something you wanted?"

"Yes." He showed Antonello how he had updated the specifications.

Antonello read them over and nodded.

"Perfetto," he said with a smile, and Chase sent them to Dewey and Dave for review and approval. It wasn't a minute before Dewey was on the phone. Chase excused himself, returning to the office to take his call.

"What is this?" Dewey asked snappily. "We had very specific specifications, and they're already changing them?"

"In a way. Their manufacturing method is something we don't do in the States, but it's better, with more built-in quality checks, and they can do it at the price they already quoted. I just updated the documentation so it reflects the method that will be used. I asked Dave to review it as well." He swallowed hard, expecting more pushback, because that was how Dewey was.

"You can't let yourself go native. You work for us, and we need these parts to be as exact as possible."

Chase was glad he wasn't on video as he flipped Dewey the bird. A familiar chuckle from his doorway told him that Antonello had seen him. "You sent me here to work with Glorioso, and that's what I'm doing." He kept calm. "If you read the document, you'll see that there are a number of quality assurance and testing steps built into the process—more than we originally asked for."

"Oh." That caught him off guard. "Well, then, if Dave agrees, we'll approve it, but this had better work, or you'll be the one whose head is on the line." He hung up, and Chase flipped him the bird once more. In fact, he used both hands.

"You could have just read what I sent you. But then that would mean that you actually had the ability to read beyond a first-grade level. Jackass." He took a deep breath and settled back in the chair. "Sorry. Did you need something?"

"One hell of a first day, isn't it?"

Chase nodded and checked the time. It was already two, and he had no doubt that he was going to get a number of additional phone calls that day.

"We could go get some lunch," Antonello offered. Chase tried to find a way to demur but couldn't think of anything off the top of his head. Besides, Ricky wasn't here, and what could a lunch hurt?

Chapter 6

"WHERE DO you usually eat?" Chase asked.

"There's a lot around. In the center of the city, most of the restaurants there are designed around tourism. The ones here are for businesspeople." He led Chase to a small restaurant with four tables. He loved this place and walked past the line of half a dozen people outside.

"Are we going to be able to get back in time?"

Antonello held the door and went back to one of the small tables against the side wall. "Sure. This is my table at lunch. I pay so it's always available." He sat down and motioned Chase to the other seat. Maria hurried over and greeted him with a kiss on each cheek.

"Ciao," she said happily before greeting Chase the same way. Antonello smiled as Chase tensed a little, not quite sure what was happening.

"This is Chase, a friend of mine from college. He is working with us on a project."

"Good. I bring you something excellent," she said, switching to English when he did. Then she patted his cheek and hurried off.

"Does she kiss all her customers on the cheeks?" Chase asked.

Antonello smiled. "Of course not. Maria was my second nanny. She looked after me from the time I was eight until I was twelve and ready to go away to school. She met Luigi right after that. He was a chef in the city, and they opened this restaurant eight years ago. I keep a table here to support them and make sure I can get their cooking whenever I want it."

"What are we getting?" Chase asked, looking around the cozy space.

"Whatever is good," Antonello answered. "Whatever it is will be amazing. Maria was always really good in the kitchen. She used to sneak down and make me her special *gnudi di spinaci* whenever the cook was busy." She returned with a bottle of wine and poured them each a glass and then hurried away before returning with two bowls of dumplings with spinach in a butter sauce. Instantly Antonello was transported back to a time when he always knew he was cared for.

"Your favorite," she said happily to Antonello, and Chase took a bite and moaned softly. "You like?" she asked, and Chase nodded, his eyes wide. Maria beamed. "I always make to get you to tell me your secrets."

Antonello always felt like he belonged whenever he was here. This place and this woman exuded comfort and care to him.

"So what secrets did you tell her?" Chase asked, raising his eyebrows.

"The kind of things that were so important when you're ten, like the fact that Pietro Brundo was bullying me at school. I was so ashamed. But as soon as I told Maria, I felt better, and she told me how to stand up to him."

Chase turned to Maria. "What was your advice?"

She leaned over the table. "I told him to get friends together and give him taste of own medicine." She smiled. "And it work." She straightened up, standing tall. "You eat. I come back later." She went to help other tables as Chase groaned once more.

"This is so good," Chase said before covering his mouth with his hand. He swallowed, and that smile grew even wider. "Oh my God. Ricky would love this."

Antonello ate, happy he'd brought Chase here. Maria stopped over a few more times to refill their wineglasses.

"I could never have wine with lunch at home."

"I know. Americans are so prudish about some things. What does a glass or two of wine hurt? We aren't going to get drunk, and wine goes with the food. What are we supposed to have, Coke? With this?" He shrugged and loved that Chase nodded across from him.

"If my boss found out…," Chase whispered.

"Then we won't tell him." Antonello put his napkin on the table, and after saying goodbye to Maria and Luigi, they left and headed back to the office.

"You always manage to lead me into trouble," Chase said.

Antonello chuckled because he was so right. Antonello had thought of himself as untouchable in college. He did everything he shouldn't have, and he dragged Chase and Elaine along with him. They always had a good time and wiggled out of their scrapes with little damage because Chase somehow always managed to talk their way out of it. And the few times he'd failed, Antonello had slipped into Italian and played the "I don't speak English" card.

"We had fun, yes?" Antonello said, knowing he certainly had. Those years with Chase and his sister were the happiest he had ever had. He still wished he had been more honest about himself and who he was. He had loved both Chase and Elaine, but because he had been denying part of himself, he had let his love of Elaine go too far, and once he'd become intimately involved with her, he didn't know how to back away without hurting her, especially since it had been Chase that he really wanted. But leaving her for her brother would have devastated Elaine, and Antonello couldn't have done it. So, like many things in his life, he had done what he knew he had to do and kept his true feelings to himself. Not that he could have acted on them anyway; his family would never have understood.

"We did," Chase agreed softly, a wistful look in his eyes. "But that was back in college." His expression grew hard. "Then you left, and Elaine and I had to pick up the pieces of our dreams and move on." His steps grew more rigid. "I don't think it's good for us to go over what happened. We agreed to be professional and work together."

Antonello knew what he'd done, and if he had the chance, he'd like to think he'd do things differently. Back then things had seemed so black and white, but maybe if he had tried harder, he could have figured out a way to have the life he wanted and make his family happy. "I know what I did, and I wish that things would have been different." He stopped just down the block from the office. "I had to come back. I'm the heir to all of this... to hundreds of years of history."

Chase put his hands on his hips. "I know that. I understand that part. What I don't get is why you weren't honest with us in the first place. You knew your family history and what was expected—you had to. Instead, we made plans and purchased things to start the business. We had commitments that all fell apart when you left. Elaine and I didn't have the resources alone to get things started. You left, and we had to take everything apart." Chase shot daggers at him.

"I didn't understand all that. I was a kid away at college, and I had started to dream my own dreams. Maybe I was foolish to think they could come true. I was told what they expected and given a choice. Come home immediately or we will cut you off. Just like that, I was ordered back." He shook his head because it sounded so feeble, even to him. Chase was right. He should have known, or at the very least have figured that shit out. He knew the traditions in his family, but like all kids, he thought the rules didn't apply to him. "I'm not going to say that I didn't have a choice, because I did. I could have stayed in the US and walked away from my family...." He swallowed hard.

"I don't think I could have done that either. But that doesn't excuse that you should have known that you couldn't stay. You should have been honest with us. And when you left, you didn't just leave Elaine and me in a lurch because of the business—you left us… you left Elaine, and she—" Chase cut himself off midsentence, and Antonello wondered what he had been about to say. "You broke her heart."

Antonello knew he had hurt her. "I know, and what am I supposed to do about it?" He had been a stupid kid and acceded to what his family demanded of him. Had he done the right thing? Probably, yes, but he had most definitely done things the wrong way, and now he was going to regret how he had left for the rest of his life.

Chase shrugged. "There's nothing you can do now. She's gone, and any chance you had to make things right with her is long past." He glared fire at Antonello, and frankly Antonello couldn't blame him. He had been stupid back then in so many ways, and now he was stuck with the consequences.

"If you really want to go there, then judging by the fact that she had Ricky with someone else, she must have gotten over me." All this angst and emotion was beginning to seem over the top. Yeah, he had left, and Chase kept blaming him for Elaine's broken heart, but there had to be something more to it. He had also stepped out on a business that hadn't even gotten off the ground. As far as he was concerned, it had just been in the idea and formation stage, but like so many things back then, he had misread the situation.

Chase seemed a little startled and paled as he blinked.

"What is it? What am I missing?" Antonello pressed. "I know there is something." Chase cleared his throat, speechless for a few seconds, which made Antonello even more curious. "You're going to have to tell me eventually. We're going to be working together for months. Do you want whatever is at the heart of this hanging over us for all that time?"

Chase nodded. "Let's just say that Elaine wasn't the only one you left behind who loved you." He turned and quickly strode down the walk to the building. By the time Antonello got over the shock of what he'd heard, Chase had pulled open the door and disappeared from sight.

He finally got his feet moving, returning to the office so he could get Chase to explain what he meant, but he was greeted by a closed door. He thought about knocking but went to his own office instead. He had plenty of work to finish, and yet he thought about the connecting door, which was just as closed and seemed as impenetrable as the other one. Part of him wanted to go in and have it out, but that was a bad idea and he knew it. He was not going to have that kind of fight in the office. Word would get back to his father, and that was the last thing Antonello wanted. This was work, and he needed to be professional. And Chase in essence telling him that he loved him all those years ago was not something to talk about here.

That revelation cast plenty about his past in a different light. Chase had loved him. Antonello sat in his chair, looking at the door to the other office. Antonello had been so unsure of his feelings back then. He knew he had them, but he'd buried them deep. There were a few times when he had cozied up to Chase, especially when he'd had too much to drink. God, he remembered a weekend when Elaine had been gone and he and Chase had bought a couple cases of something called PBR. Cheap beer that tasted better after the third one. After a while, he lost track of what he drank, and he and Chase ended up curled together on the sofa, laughing until Chase fell asleep draped over him, his shirt riding up, giving Antonello a long look at his flat belly. He had longed to touch, to hold Chase in his arms, to see what he tasted like, and for a second, he had almost done just that. He wanted to badly, and he'd leaned forward to get closer to Chase's lips, getting that first touch of a kiss, but he misbalanced and fell off the sofa, taking Chase with him. Both of them ended up on the floor in a fit of giggles. Chase managed to get himself to bed somehow while Antonello woke the following morning on the sofa, wondering if that moment had really happened. Chase never mentioned it, and Antonello figured that was best and began dating Elaine shortly afterward, if only to prove to himself that his moment of weakness had been the beer and nothing more.

A buzz intruded on his thoughts. It came again, snapping him back to the present. He picked up the phone, remembering that the past was little more than a minefield and he needed to keep his thoughts in the present.

"ARE YOU going to be able to work with him, this American?" his father asked before sipping his Aperol. "Is this going to be good for us?"

"Yes." Antonello nodded. "I knew him in college. He and I were friends before I returned here." He set his glass aside, not thirsty. "He and his sister were my closest friends while I was there. It's nice to see him again." He kept his expression bland because his mother could read him like a book, and he did not want to answer her questions. "Anyway, I think we will work well together and that the deal could be very good for us."

"Excellent," his father said.

His mother watched him with the eyes of a hawk. "You were seen outside the store, talking to a man with a little boy."

"That was Chase. He and his nephew were shopping for a present for Chase's mother, and they stopped in the shop."

"Did you give them a good price?" his father asked.

Antonello smiled. "Of course I did. I want this to be a good relationship that will last beyond this one contract." His father seemed satisfied.

But not his mother. "You were also seen around town with them."

"Contessina, he's being a good host. They will be working together, and you know that building long-lasting relationships is how we grow the business in the long run. Antonello is doing exactly what I would do in this situation. Spending time outside of work with this man and his son will make it easier to do business, especially if there is a problem. Then they can work it out." He sat back, sipping his drink. His father was the only person who could counter his mother when she got curious. But if Antonello thought she was through, he was mistaken.

"I was talking to Mary Gianetti today, and she has a daughter about your age. She showed me a picture. Giulia is pretty, and her mother says that she is wonderful. You should meet her. It's time for you to get married and have children." This wasn't the first time his mother had tried to push one of her friends' daughters off on him. "You need to get married so you can have a son to carry on the family. Your cousin has a wife, and your aunt tells me that they're working to have a child."

"They are?" He rolled his eyes. "Then why is Lorenzo walking through town with a tourist from Spain? I met her the other day when he brought her to the store." He hoped that little bit of information would put his mother off what had become her favorite topic lately.

"You didn't let him get anything, did you?" his father asked a little forcefully. It didn't escape Antonello's notice that neither of his parents were surprised. Lorenzo didn't think marriage should preclude him from spending time with other women.

"Of course not. I told Renate and Claudio, and they were more than happy to make sure he doesn't try to go around us."

His father nodded, and it seemed he had put his mother off her game just enough that he got a few minutes' respite from her matchmaking.

"Good," his father said.

"Aria deserves better than your cousin," Mother said softly. "She's a nice girl and a good wife. Luigi, you need to make sure your sister knows so she can do something about that son of hers." Antonello did not want to be Lorenzo once his aunt found out about her son's latest escapade. "If you treat your wife that way…." His mother's voice grew deeper, the warning crystal clear. Antonello cleared his throat, knowing she was warming up to her favorite subject. "I hear that Margaretta Venutti is back. She went away to America for school like you did. And I know she's single."

Antonello turned to his father. This was becoming a common theme with his mother, and he was tired of it.

"Contessina, leave him alone. He doesn't need you to find him a wife. Our son is handsome, and any woman would be lucky to have him. He will find his own wife, just like I found you."

His mother scoffed. "I'm the one who found you."

"True. But do you remember who my mother wanted me to marry?" His father chuckled.

His mother smiled softly. "Gemma Vesta," his mother said. "She would have been all wrong for you, and the last I heard, she buried her second husband after nagging him to death. Guido gave up living rather than spend another day with her." She sipped from her glass. "But I have better taste than your mother, and I know my son and what he needs."

"He does not need to marry the daughter of Mary Gianetti. The girl is pretty, but in twenty years she will start to look like her mother." Dad's eyes sparkled. Mary Gianetti had a face only a mother could love. It was a good thing her husband, Carlo, was nearly blind.

"I will find the right person for me," Antonello said. "And I'm not going to choose anyone you pick out for me. I will get married and have children in my own time. Couples are waiting to get married and have children. I'm not in a hurry."

"You should be. The goods girls will all be snapped up, and then you'll be left with the Gemma Vestas of the world." She shot him a firm look, daring Antonello to try to tell her that she was wrong. "I'm your mother, and I know these things."

"But that doesn't mean that I want you choosing my wife for me." More than anything, he wanted this conversation to end, and thankfully, his father asked his mother about her work with the Amici degli Uffizi, the group that supported the famous museum, which effectively changed the subject. But he knew it was only a temporary reprieve. His mother never gave up on anything without a fight.

Chapter 7

"Ricky!" Chase called when he got home that evening, happy to be out of the office and away from Antonello. On the work front, it had been very productive. Dave was reviewing the updates to the specifications to ensure that the changes in production methodology would truly be beneficial. Chase thought they would be, but a second opinion was warranted, with so much on the line.

"Guncle Daddy," Ricky called, giggling as he raced across the room and into his arms. Then he began speaking in Italian, saying something Chase didn't understand. "Now, you say, 'Com'è andata la tua?'" Chase repeated the words, and Ricky answered. The only word he caught in his response was *gelato*.

"What does all that mean?"

"I asked how your day was, and you asked about mine, and then I told you that Bianca and I learned more Italian and got gelato. It was yummy." He smiled widely, and Chase held him tightly.

"I will go now," Bianca said. "See you tomorrow," she told Ricky, who waved.

"Ciao, bella," Ricky said as they saw her to the door. Chase thanked her for watching Ricky and closed the door behind her.

Ricky chattered away as he held him. Chase closed his eyes, his heart racing as he did his best not to let Ricky see his distress. He had been so close to spilling the beans about Ricky. The words were on the tip of his tongue, and he had only stopped himself at the last second. On top of that, he had nearly come out and told Antonello how he felt. What a mess. He rocked Ricky in his arms, hoping like hell he could keep it together. Yes, he was angry with Antonello for what he'd done, but he was more upset with himself.

He kept telling himself that he didn't know for sure if Ricky was Antonello's son, but the more he looked, the more he could see it. And he was absolutely shocked that Antonello *didn't* see it. But at least he could breathe more easily on that score. If he thought Elaine had moved on after he left, then that should help keep Antonello from suspecting himself as Ricky's father.

But that was only one part of the minefield his life had become. Chase had really hoped that Antonello would have turned into a real asshole. That would make keeping him at a distance so easy. But he was the same person Chase had known in college. Back then, Chase had been too reticent to express his feelings. He'd simply kept them to himself.

"Daddy, you look sad," Ricky said.

"I don't mean to," Chase told him, forcing the worry away and himself to smile. "What should we have for dinner?"

"Pesto," Ricky said exuberantly.

"Do you know what that is?" Chase asked.

"Green pasta. It's good. Bianca made it." He squirmed, and Chase put him down. Ricky ran to the small refrigerator and pulled it open, then pointed to a plastic container inside. "We cooked together. She makes yummy stuff, and she showed me how to put in the olive oil and the green stuff, and I stirred it." He seemed so proud.

Apparently Bianca was a lifesaver. "Yes, we can have the pesto that you made." He pulled out the container and put it in the microwave before getting out the plates and silverware for dinner. Ricky had already climbed into his place at the table, and by the time dinner was hot, he had everything else ready to go. He dished up some for his son and then put some on his plate.

"You still look sad," Ricky said.

"I'm just busy right now." His mind kept whirling through things with Antonello. What he really needed was to just go back home. His life was simpler back in Harrisburg, and he wasn't in this constant state of worry and wonder.

"Did you see Mr. Nello?" Ricky got a piece of pasta on his fork and blew on it. "He was nice. Can we see him again? I liked him."

"Maybe." The last thing he wanted was Antonello and Ricky in the same place. "Now eat your pasta." It was really good, and Chase was both surprised and pleased that Ricky liked it. Thankfully he wasn't a picky eater and seemed willing to try new things.

Once they were finished with dinner, Chase got Ricky his bath and then ready for bed. After reading him a story and turning out the light, he kissed his son good night and closed the door to his room. Then he settled in a chair with his laptop. He intended to work for a while but ended up watching something on Netflix before getting ready for bed.

He messaged his mom to say good night before turning out the lights, but stared up at the colored plaster ceiling. He hadn't wanted to come here. His past with Antonello was difficult enough, but now that history seemed to have taken on a life of its own and was making itself felt in the present. He should have gotten past what happened after college, but it was more difficult than he had expected. Feelings he thought had long been buried kept coming to the surface, and just like in college, he didn't know what to do with them. He knew acting on them would be a bad idea, but every time he was in the room with Antonello, he found it hard not to watch him. His heart beat a little faster, and he could swear Antonello could warm a room just by walking in.

There had always been something about him that drew Chase, always. Back then, their friendship had stopped him from acting on it. And now he had a job to do and Ricky to think about. Chase rolled onto his side, punching the pillow in a futile effort to get comfortable. His mother would have a fit and his sister would roll over in her grave, but if he were honest with himself, Chase had always wanted Antonello. He wasn't just handsome—unlike a lot of others in his life, Antonello had always listened to him and paid attention to him.

He wasn't going to get any answers at the moment, and the darkness wasn't going to provide any grand revelations. Elaine had always told him that he was the worrying twin. "You need to stop wondering what could have happened or what will happen and just enjoy what does happen." He tried to remember the number of times she had told him that. And she was right. Chase always worried about everything, and most of the time, his efforts were wasted.

One thing he did know: Ricky liked Antonello, and that said a lot for him. Ricky was a great kid who had good people instincts. The truth—something he could only admit to himself here, alone in his room—was that he had loved Antonello back in college, and those feelings were roaring back. The question was what, if anything, he was going to do about them. Logic told him to do nothing, but part of him was desperate to know if Antonello might feel the same.

"DADDY, WHAT are we going to do today?" Ricky asked the following Saturday morning. Chase and Antonello had come to a working peace, with Antonello being friendly but professional for the rest of the week.

The specifications had been reviewed and the updates approved, so next week they'd move to initial prototype production preparations. But for now all Chase wanted was to rest.

"It's a little after seven in the morning," Chase said as Ricky settled under the covers next to him. His son always had trouble sleeping if it was light out, and Chase made a note to get better curtains for Ricky's room or he was never going to be able to sleep in the rest of the time they were here.

"I'm awake and I wanna do stuff. Bianca showed me pictures of the naked stone man. Can we see that?" Ricky leaned close, whispering. "You could see his penis and everything." He giggled, and Chase wondered how he was going to explain the styles of Renaissance sculpture to Ricky.

"That's David, and I don't think so. Not today. Though we can go to the Accademia another day if you really want." He could just imagine what Ricky would say when they did visit. Good Lord.

"Are there other naked people there?" Ricky asked, and Chase groaned.

"How about you try to go back to sleep and not worry about the statues? I'll tell you all about it and what it means later." *Preferably when you're an adult.* "Daddy needs some more sleep. Okay?" He closed his eyes, and Ricky thankfully settled down… until Chase's phone vibrated on the table beside the bed.

"Daddy, the phone is shaking," Ricky said as though it was something important.

Chase reached for it and groaned. It wasn't even eight in the morning, so what could Antonello want?

"Yeah," he answered groggily. "Is something wrong?"

"No. But I managed to make arrangements for you and Ricky. I'll be outside your place in ten minutes." He sounded damned pleased with himself.

"Is that Mr. Nello?" Ricky asked as Antonello hung up.

"Yes. He's coming over. We need to get dressed." And Chase needed coffee—lots of coffee.

"For gelato?" Ricky asked.

God, he hoped not. "I think it's too early for that. Go put on the clothes I laid out for you last night so we can be dressed when he gets here." Ten freaking minutes. Antonello obviously had no idea what it took to get a six-year-old ready for the day. Still, Ricky raced away, and

Chase shaved and dressed before finding Ricky in his room, clothes and shoes on with the Velcro done up. He sat on the side of his bed, looking at Chase like he was wondering what took him so long.

"I even brushed teeth," he said, showing them to Chase with a big grin. "Is he here yet?"

"Not yet." He held out his hand, and Ricky took it. Then they went to the kitchen, where he got Ricky something quick to eat and gave him a glass of juice. Chase was too curious to eat, but Ricky ate his grapes and toast, drinking the last of his juice as the bell rang.

"He's here!" Ricky hurried to the door as Chase set the dishes in the sink. "I'm ready, Guncle Daddy," he sang. "Can we go?"

"Yes." He was getting excited as well and took Ricky's hand, meeting Antonello at the door. They left, and he locked up on the way out before they stepped into the quiet street, which got busier as they approached the center of the historic city.

"Where are we going?" Ricky asked, practically dancing with excitement.

Antonello pointed upward. "There." Chase followed where he was pointing to the top of the cathedral.

Ricky clapped his hands as he shouted with glee. "Really? All the way to the top?"

"All the way up there." He smiled. "I have a friend who works there, and he is going to get us in before they open." Antonello's happy gaze shifted to Chase. "Sorry for the fast notice. Tourists go up starting at nine, so we had to get here quickly."

Chase looked upward for a moment, his belly churning at the thought of being that far off the ground. He didn't want to think about it too much. Just the idea made him cold. But dammit, Ricky wanted to go so bad, and Chase wasn't going to tell him no because of his own fear of heights.

"Do we go in there?" Ricky asked as they passed the front door of the building, where people were already lined up to get inside.

"Nope. It's over here," Antonello said, leading them around to the side, where a shorter line had formed. Antonello led them right to the front and spoke to the man in Italian. He nodded and opened the door, and the three of them went inside. "There are lots of stairs."

"I can do it, and so can Daddy," Ricky said. "I'll help you if your legs are tired."

Chase smiled and took Ricky's hand. "We'll do it together," he said with more confidence than he felt as they took the first steps into a gray stone stairway that circled upward and back around on itself.

"These stairs were put in way back when the building was built, over five hundred years ago. So be careful. They have worn over the centuries after thousands of people have used them," Antonello explained.

It was enclosed, and some of Chase's worry slipped away as they came to a small room. "Is this it?"

"This is the top of the outside wall." Antonello led them inward to more steps, and they continued their upward trek before going through another door and stepping out onto an interior walkway at the base of the dome. Chase took one look down and froze solid.

"Daddy?" Ricky asked around the edge of his hearing.

"Chase, it's okay. Look up. Those paintings on the dome are masterpieces, and you get to see them up close." He lifted his gaze up into the dome just over his head. "Take my hand. We just have to get to that next door."

He nodded, getting Ricky in front of him. Antonello stayed behind him, holding his other hand. Chase squeezed it and took his first step, concentrating on the walkway and the paintings above him rather than the long way down with death waiting at the bottom. Fuck, he hated heights, and he couldn't help thinking about what would happen if he fell.

"Daddy, it's so pretty up here," Ricky said as he peered over the railing. "I love it. All the seats and the pretty floor."

"Just keep going," Chase managed to say without shouting, even though he wanted to scream at Antonello to get him out of there. Still, he kept moving forward until they got to the next doorway. He stepped through into yet another passage with stairs that led around the side of the dome. And the damned things went higher. Chase took a deep breath, squeezed Antonello's hand tightly, and took the first step.

"We're between the inner and outer domes. The outer one is what you see from the outside, and the one inside has the paintings you looked at." Antonello stopped. "See the brick pattern? That's part of what makes it stay up and why it's strong." He patted the wall. "You're seeing Renaissance workmanship right in front of your eyes." They continued upward and came to a stop where a man stood.

"Watch your step as you go up, and take it slow." Ricky went right up the steps that curved along the top of the dome. Chase went after him, breathing steadily as he climbed, with Antonello behind him. He forced himself to go upward until he passed through a door in the ceiling and out into fresh air and what might as well have been the fiery pits of hell, six hundred feet in the air.

Chase took Ricky's hand, backed up against the side of the lantern at the very top of the dome, and stood there, refusing to move.

"Look how pretty it is," Ricky said and then gasped. "There's the Ponty bridge, and, oh look, all those people down there." He waved and stepped forward.

"It's all right," Antonello said softly from next to him. "You should have told me."

"I'll be okay," Chase said, forcing air into his lungs and opening his eyes. The initial panic subsided, and he looked from side to side, the city laid out below. "Would you take Ricky so he can see everything? I'll stay right here."

"Hey, it's okay. Just give yourself a few minutes. This dome and the floor you're standing on have been here, standing tall, for over five hundred years." He entwined his fingers with Chase's, and slowly, the realization that they were holding hands and how good it felt pressed forward in his mind, diluting his fear. The tightness in his chest faded away, and Chase turned to Antonello, bathed in reassurance from those amazingly deep eyes. "Nothing is going to happen to you. I promise." He drew closer, and Chase nodded, concentrating on Antonello's touch.

For a moment, Chase forgot where he was, his mind centered on the touch of Antonello's hand and the way their legs brushed together. Ricky held his other hand. "Daddy, are you gonna woof?"

Chase smiled and even chuckled. "No. I'm not."

"Then let's go. There's lots to see." He tugged lightly at his hand.

"Just give me another minute." The floor wasn't falling from under him, and Antonello had his hand, and whenever he opened his eyes, the amazing city spread out below, and his old friend was right there, steadying him.

"See the ring of stone under your feet? You don't need to step off that. Just slowly move around and Ricky can see everything." Antonello slowly guided them around the lantern. Ricky chattered on about everything he was seeing, and Chase smiled, loving the happiness in his voice.

"There's where we live. Look, Daddy," Ricky cried with delight, and Chase let himself follow to where he pointed.

"Yup. That's our building, and there's the Pitti Palace that we visited. And the Palazzo Vecchio."

"We can go there sometime if you want. It has hidden passages in the walls that we can go through," Antonello told Ricky, who vibrated with excitement. "There's even a whole hidden room that no one knew about for a very long time. When they found it, there was a table and chairs, but all the cloth had disintegrated where it sat because no one had been inside for hundreds of years."

"Can we go? Now?" Ricky asked.

"How about we enjoy the view from up here, and then we can get something to eat once my feet are back on solid ground." Chase followed Antonello and Ricky as they made their way all the way around. Others joined them on the cupola as the first group of tourists reached the top, their voices jarring against the quiet of just the wind and Ricky's laughter. "Should we go down?" Chase asked once they returned to where they started.

"Can we get a picture?" Antonello asked.

"Yeah, Daddy," Ricky said, standing next to him. Antonello pulled out his phone, and Chase smiled for the camera.

"Can you take one of your daddy and me?" Antonello asked, and Ricky grinned.

"Yes!"

Chase unlocked his phone and brought up the camera, then handed it to Ricky. Then Antonello lightly tugged him away from the wall so they stood together.

"The view is stunning," Antonello said, and Chase realized he was looking right at him. His intense gaze never wavered as his lips curled upward. For a second Antonello leaned closer, and Chase wondered if he was going to close the distance between them right there at what felt like the top of the world. "And I mean it," Antonello added as Ricky took the pictures and then lowered the phone.

Chase didn't move, lost in a spell he had dreamed of long ago but never thought could possibly come about. He had always wondered if Antonello had been flirting with him in college, and all these years later, he had a definitive answer. The desire in his eyes shone brightly, and Chase completely forgot where he was, lost in a gaze he had longed for.

"Are you going to kiss? If you do, I'll look away, because that's yucky."

Chase groaned, and Antonello backed away, the moment broken. Antonello cleared his throat. "You should give your daddy back his phone and we can go back down."

Chase nodded, and once he had stowed his phone, one of the attendants helped him down through the door and over the dome. Once he was on the walkway, he held Ricky's hand, and they went back down the way they came until they reached the walkway inside the dome. They made their way to the far side of the cathedral and finally down two more winding staircases to the ground, with Antonello silent the entire way, and Chase wondering what he should do to regain the surprising ease he had felt back at the top.

Chapter 8

"THAT WAS so cool," Ricky said as he practically danced along, holding Chase's hand as they waded through the throngs of people who now filled the square. "I could see everything." He grinned as Antonello turned to Chase, who looked back.

"I'm sorry. If I had known you didn't like heights, I…."

"Once I got used to being up there, it wasn't so bad, and the view is amazing," Chase said, making Antonello wonder what he had done. Chase had turned off on the way down, and Antonello hadn't known what to say. Maybe he'd pushed too hard and should have offered to take Ricky up and let Chase stay below.

"Can we get gelato?" Ricky asked.

"It's too early, and you only had toast and juice at home." He checked the time as the bell in the tower began chiming ten.

"I know just the place if you're hungry," Antonello offered, hoping Chase would accept. "It's just over there." He led them away from the square and down a side street to a small café. They sat down, and a woman came out, smiling.

"It's about time you came to see me," she chided lightly in Italian. "Who are your friends?"

Antonello switched to English. "This is Chase and his son, Ricky. I went to school in America with him, and he's now working with us for a few months. This is Isabella, and these two are her sons, Gerardo and Santo." The two boys, slightly older than Ricky, smiled before hurrying down the street with a ball.

"Do you want to go too?" she asked Ricky and called after the boys.

"Can I?" Ricky asked.

"They won't go far," Isabella explained, and Chase nodded. Ricky raced off, and the boys began some sort of game with the ball that looked a little like three-person soccer.

"It seems some things transcend language," Chase said as all three of them played and laughed a ways away. "I want him to make new friends."

"They are good boys, and they learn English in school," Isabella told Chase. "They figure it out." She smiled and took their orders for coffee before returning inside.

"What has you so uptight, as we used to say?" Antonello asked.

"Nothing."

"Liar," Antonello said without heat. "I know you, remember? I can tell when you're inside your head. Elaine used to call you out on it all the time. So what has your head churning?"

"I don't know. I guess the way you… flirted. The way you did that in college. For years I thought I was seeing things. But I wasn't, and then you started dating Elaine, and I really thought it was just me."

"Are you wondering if I cared for Elaine? Because I did. She was amazing and always had that way of looking at things that made the worst situation better." He really missed that about her.

Chase nodded slowly. "But I guess…." He stopped when Isabella returned with their coffee and a plate of pastries and a few cookies. Then she called to the boys to stay close and returned inside the café. Antonello sipped his coffee, waiting for Chase to continue. "I'm wondering what the deal is."

"The deal?" Sometimes he still got confused by English sayings.

"Your deal. Do you like girls, boys?"

Antonello nodded and then shrugged. "I guess I'm gay… as you call it. But don't think I didn't love Elaine. I did, and she's the only woman I have ever been with." Just saying the words to someone felt so good, like lifting a weight off his chest, and he knew Chase would understand, even if no one else in his life would. "My family does not know, and my mother is starting to push her friends' daughters into my path. But I'm not interested in them." He lowered his voice and stopped talking when he heard footsteps.

Isabella returned and called to the boys, who all ran over like she was the Pied Piper. She gave them each some cookies. Ricky tasted his and then wolfed the rest down. Then they ran back to their games and Isabella returned inside.

"I see. You're in the closet."

"Yes. I am, and I know it. My father will never understand, and you know that. I have a duty here, the same one that pulled me home instead of us going into business together, which is what I wanted to do." He sipped his coffee. "The business has been in my family for hundreds of years and always passed from father to son. If I have no children, then the business would pass to my cousin and his line of the family."

"Which would be bad?" Chase asked.

It would be a disaster. "After you left, he came to the store the other day with a tourist from Spain. He wanted to use his family discount. I took that opportunity to remind him about his wife and that she would cut off his nuts if she knew. That's my cousin. He thinks of nothing other than what he wants right now. Not the future or about anyone else." He drank his coffee as he shook his head. "I like Aria, his wife. She is very nice and too good for him. Aria also has a temper, and I wouldn't want to cross her. But she has a blind spot where Lorenzo is concerned."

"I see. So you came home to rescue the family business from him, and you still have to have a son or your cousin could be the one to carry on the family legacy." Chase sipped his coffee, watching the boys play. "What I don't understand is, what about you? What do you want? When you talk about the future, you always speak of duty and family expectations, but what about your life? Does anyone care about what would make you happy?"

Antonello set down his coffee, staring across the table at Chase. That question had never occurred to him, but no. No one had ever asked what he wanted or liked. His parents always spoke of his duty and what he had to do for the family and their future. He had been drilled since he was a small child on what was expected of him and what he had to do. There had never been any questions about what he wanted. His major in college was chosen by his parents, in line with the role he was expected to fill. There had never even been any discussion about alternatives. His parents had never told him what they hoped for him and then given him a chance to choose the family or another path. There had never been a choice. That had been stripped away, and his life had been set on a path of hereditary duty and nothing else.

"You don't need to answer. I can tell by your lost expression that no one ever has." He turned to Ricky and smiled. "Except maybe Elaine and me. We had our own dreams, didn't we?" He seemed nostalgic for a few seconds, looking just like he had in college.

"We did, and I cherished those for a lot longer than I had a right to. For the record, I wanted those dreams to come true just as much as you did." He held on to them for too long because that was the only time in his life when he got to choose something for himself. "I'm sorry I screwed it all up."

Chase nodded. "Thanks for that. It may not have worked out, but it could have been so much fun to give it a shot." Their plan had been to import some of the amazing items that Antonello's family produced and sell them in their own shop. There were multiple levels of workmanship and quality in the Glorioso lines of artisan jewelry, but they had all agreed that the middle level would probably have done very well, especially in Philadelphia. Those items, unlike what was sold on the Ponte Vecchio, were machine-made, still fine quality, but with components that were decorated by hand so each was still unique. They were more affordable than the entirely handmade ones. It would have benefited the family and given all of them a future that they made themselves. It was too bad they never got the chance.

"DADDY, CAN Gerardo and Santo come over sometime?" Ricky was an amazing kid.

"I think we can arrange that." Chase hugged Ricky. "I take it you had a good time."

Ricky nodded and leaned close to his dad. "They don't have Legos, and I have lots, so we could build stuff." He nestled in close to Chase. For a second, Antonello was jealous of the boy.

"I think we can do that," Chase said. "Now you can go play for a little while more, and then we'll have lunch here before going home." He lifted his gaze. "Is that okay with you?"

"It's great. Isabella makes her own pasta, and she has a cousin on the coast who brings her fresh fish each day when he comes in for the market. I'll ask her to bring us what's special." He called, and she came out.

"Do you have a menu?"

Isabella scoffed. "I bring you what's good. Okay?" She didn't wait for an answer and went back inside.

"She told you, Daddy," Ricky said before hurrying back to where the boys were waiting.

Antonello sat back in his seat, sipping the last of his coffee, his gaze traveling to the bright blue sky above. He was calm, content, and even happy. It had been a long time since he felt this comfortable in his own skin.

"Antonello!" a rough voice called, and instantly he tensed as a chair scraped on the cobbled walk. "Contessina said you were out, and I figured I could find you here," Paolo said in Italian before switching to

English, sitting at the table without being asked. "How is America?" he asked Chase. "I heard there was an earthquake there. Was it near you?"

"Paolo, America is huge. So no. It was thousands of kilometers away." Antonello sighed as the tensions of his usual life flooded back. "And you can turn off your ridiculous charms. They don't have a place here, and Chase is not one of the tourists you pick up. Paolo here tells tourists that he was the model for David and then asks them if they want to go back to his place to find out."

Chase snorted, and Antonello loved that smile and the laugh. "So he isn't into brain surgeons."

"Paolo is into any woman who will let him show them a good time before they leave town in a few days with their memories… of just how pathetic a Latin lover can truly be." Paolo put his hands over his heart like he'd been mortally wounded. "That's what the last three girls you picked up told me."

"Stronzo," Paolo swore lightly.

"What does that mean?" Chase asked.

"I bet you can figure it out," Antonello said as the boys all came over, out of breath and grinning. "This is Chase's son, Ricky. Guys, this is Paolo."

"The soccer player?" Santo asked with a touch of awe. "I watched you play."

"Thanks." Paolo ruffled Santo's hair and even signed his ball when he asked. "Are you having lunch?"

"Sì. I bring enough for all of you." Isabella swiped Paolo with her cloth. "And the big shot can pay." They all laughed, and she went inside before returning with platters of food that she set on the table, followed by plates and glasses. Chase got Ricky in his seat, and Antonello brought over another table. Soon Isabella's boys settled in with them. For him, it was as close to a real family meal as he ever got… at least with the family of his heart. And like all Italian family meals, it was a bit raucous, full of laughter. It only took him three tries to get Isabella to sit down with them. The boys seemed to figure out a kind of melded conversation, and even Paolo behaved himself.

"What level did you play?" Chase asked.

"I made the national team twice and played on a World Cup and Olympic teams. But that was two years ago, and now I think I am too old. Yes? So I work in finance with my family now."

"What does that mean?" Chase asked. "Are you a banker?"

Paolo shrugged and refilled wineglasses. Antonello knew that Paolo liked to come across as playful and a bit of a playboy, but there was a serious side to him. He simply kept it very well hidden. Paolo was one of those people who loved his life and didn't see the need to talk about anything serious. "Why spoil this great lunch talking about things that are boring? Life is too short to be dull." He talked to the boys, reveling in being the soccer star.

"Do you like it?" Chase asked. He had given Ricky a small taste of everything, and he wolfed down the fish and pasta, grinning like they were the best things he had ever eaten.

"Good," Ricky said.

"Grazie," Isabella said with a huge smile, and once she finished her lunch, she switched back into restaurateur mode and began clearing the dishes for everyone else. Chase stood and began helping, following her inside.

"He's a strange one," Paolo said softly in Italian.

Antonello leaned close enough that the others couldn't hear. "He's caring, and he believes in helping rather than expecting everyone to wait on him. You could learn something."

Paolo smiled his best disarming smile, which worked on just about everyone else, but Antonello had seen it enough to know to ignore it. Chase returned and sat back down, talking softly to Ricky, who seemed to be winding down. "Can we play some more?" Ricky asked.

"Sure. If that's what you want," Chase agreed, and all three boys returned to their game.

"I should go too," Paolo said. "I have to meet someone."

"Who is it?" Antonello asked.

Paolo shrugged. "I don't know yet. But I will in a few hours." That smile was back, and after handing Isabella some money, he kissed her on the cheek and strode off like he owned the world.

Chase sipped his wine as he and Antonello watched him go. Isabella took the last of the dishes inside while they enjoyed their wine.

"Did you and he ever…?" Chase asked. "I mean, Paolo is good-looking, and…."

Antonello chuckled and shook his head but leaned closer to keep his voice low. This sort of thing was something he never spoke about, much less in a place like this. "He is all about the women and would never consider or see anything else." He couldn't help swallowing and wondering if their friendship would remain if Paolo knew about his true feelings and where his interests lay. For all his bravado and charm, Paolo liked his world ordered and easy to understand. That was part of why he dated tourists and even married women. Paolo loved women, there was no doubt of that, but he also loved simplicity, so he always saw women who would make no demands on him, just as he made none on them. Everyone had a good time and they went home, and Paolo returned to his life. Antonello often wondered what would happen when Paolo finally met someone he didn't want to let go of. "Besides, he's a friend, and I never thought of him that way. We've known each other too long. It would be like getting involved with my brother." He glanced around, glad they were alone.

"Sorry," Chase said and drank the last of the wine in his glass.

Antonello shrugged again and sat back, sipping his wine and enjoying the afternoon. He didn't often get times like this. "It's nothing." Chase watched the boys play, and Antonello watched him, maybe too much, because he caught Isabella looking at him in that knowing, motherly way she had, and he felt his belly twist a little. She patted his shoulder, leaving her hand there a little longer than necessary. Antonello relaxed, and she drew her hand away as a small group sat at one of the other tables.

Chase stood, instantly tense. Antonello followed his gaze to where Ricky sat on the ground, holding his leg. "Are you okay?" Chase called.

Ricky hurried over, showing off his scraped knee. "I fell," he said with a sniffle. "Is it bleeding?" He held it up but looked away.

"No. It's just a little pink. I can wash it when we get home." Chase hugged Ricky, who ran back to play as soon as Chase let him go. "Crisis averted."

Antonello couldn't help wishing the crises in his life could be alleviated as easily.

Chapter 9

Chase sat in the office he was using, composing an email to his ridiculous boss, who was now demanding daily updates on even the smallest things. The past two weeks had been busy, but mostly with smaller tasks and annoying busywork. It had also been two weeks spending time with Antonello and enjoying every minute, even if he wondered if he should allow himself to be happy about it. And two weeks of wondering how no one seemed to see the resemblance between Ricky and Antonello. His friends Isabella and Paolo hadn't seemed to, and others they met didn't comment. Chase was beginning to think it was his imagination. Maybe he was seeing things that weren't there, his mind filling in what it now expected.

He didn't know. When he'd first seen Ricky and Antonello together, the revelation had struck him so hard that he had been so damned sure. But maybe he'd been wrong and stupid for worrying about it so much. No one else saw it. Maybe it was just him.

"The first set of prototypes have been sent to your office for testing," Antonello said after knocking on the door between their offices and striding inside with that confident air that made him seem taller and his eyes just a little brighter. Chase had seen few things hotter than a confident Antonello.

"I thought they weren't supposed to be ready for another week." Chase looked up from his email to Dewey. He had always known his boss wasn't the brightest bulb on the string, but he was at least supposed to be qualified and knowledgeable about the company's products. Now the more Chase worked with him, the more certain he was that Dewey had been skating by for years.

"It wasn't. But we had a delay in another project, so I put the guys to work on this one and they got it done. All the settings have been saved, so as long as we get approval, we can move into initial production. Our people here are testing as well to make sure the pieces supplied meet the specifications, but I figured your team would want to do their own analysis."

Chase grinned and picked up the phone. It was late in the day, so Dave should be in the office back home. "Hey, some initial prototypes are on the way for you and the team to look at. So you'll need to watch for them." He looked at Antonello, who mouthed Dave's name. Perfect. "I want to stress that testing hasn't been done here yet, but they figured you would want to look them over as well."

"That's great." Dave lowered his voice. "I'll keep my mouth shut and let you give the boss the heads-up." That was a change. Dave never referred to Dewey as *boss*. Something was going on. "You deserve to give him the good news."

"Thanks. I'm just sending him his daily update now."

"Good. Maybe that will get him off the warpath," Dave groused.

"I see." Chase pulled the phone away and spoke softly to Antonello. "Can I come to your office in a little while?"

Antonello nodded and left the room.

"What's going on?" he asked Dave.

Dave paused, and Chase heard a door close. "Apparently Dewey's boss is starting to question Dewey's abilities, and this project is his final lifeline. If it goes south…. Well, you know, and he's been awful to everyone. Instead of getting the team to pull together, he's yanking and pulling at everyone, and they're feeling the pressure. And I suspect some of his shit is going to be coming your way. So watch out and tread carefully."

Just what he needed. "Thanks."

"I'm serious. He is going to see this project as his possible savior and a huge feather in his cap, so expect him to want to know and try to understand every detail, even if he isn't capable of it." Damn, Dave rarely spoke this bluntly. Chase had always thought Dewey and Dave were close, but it seemed he was wrong. Either that or the scales had fallen from Dave's eyes. In any event, he had no intention of saying a thing in case the wind changed.

"I got it. I need to make a few more calls before the end of business here. Call me when the package arrives."

Dave agreed and ended the call.

Chase took a deep breath and called Dewey.

"What? You better not have a problem," Dewey growled.

"The first prototypes have been readied and will go out tomorrow. Dave is expecting them and will get them over to our team. They had a schedule change and were able to get a small initial run completed. Glorioso will be testing along with us."

"Good. That's good." He paused. "I want you to go through all your schedules and tighten them up. If this came in early, then there must be slack in other places."

"Dewey, we got this early only because another Glorioso client postponed their delivery by a week. We took their slot, and they'll take ours. The rest of the schedule isn't fluid." He stood and pulled open the connecting door to Antonello's office, never so happy for a door like that in his life.

"Is that what they said?" Dewey snapped.

"Hold on a minute." He covered the phone. "My boss is trying to push everything up because of the early delivery. I need you to explain that nothing else can shift."

Antonello stood and came into his office and shut the door. "No problem."

"Dewey, I'm putting you on speaker." He shifted the phone. "I'm here with Antonello Glorioso."

"Good day, Dewey," Antonello said formally. "We have a very tight schedule for our production. It is committed for months in advance. A longtime customer asked if it would be possible for us to delay production for a week because of other supply issues on their end, so we upped the initial work for your prototypes. They will go out tomorrow." Antonello was calm and totally businesslike.

"What about the rest of the schedule?"

"That is unaffected. This will simply give our teams more time for testing and verification. Final approval must be complete by the date already specified."

"But I want to move the timeline forward," Dewey snapped.

"We will not be able to do that," Antonello said levelly, which had to drive Dewey up a tree. He hated for anyone to tell him no. "Timelines and detail schedules were already agreed upon and signed off… by you. We intend to stick with them, and there is little we can do unless something unforeseen arises. And if it does, I will be sure to let Chase know right away." Antonello stood. "I have a meeting in ten minutes. I hope you have a good rest of your day." He left the office, closing the door, and Chase picked up the phone.

"That guy is a real piece of work. What would his boss say about his attitude?"

Chase smiled. "You mean his father?" He loved asking that question. "Antonello is the heir to the company and all his family's businesses, so I don't think we can go any farther up the ladder."

Dewey was silent for a few minutes. "You need to remember that you work for us and not them. We need to try to push this project up and make it a success."

Chase shook his head. "The only way that can happen is if we get our verification and testing done early and sign off on it. Then, if they have an opening, we can get the next set of parts, build devices, and submit them to the FDA for testing. After that, we can go to the trials. This is a long process. You know that. So we take it one step at a time, make sure it's right and successful, and then we can move on." He kept his tone soft and his mounting frustration out of it. "Any shortcuts could endanger the entire project." This seemed rote. Dewey knew all of this. This kind of project took years, not days or months. The FDA worked on its own timeline, and yet Dewey was worried about pushing up the timeline of a single part by a few weeks.

"I need things to happen faster," Dewey pressed. Chase remained quiet. There was nothing more he could do, and in situations like this, it was best to keep quiet, not promise anything, and let Dewey work out his own issues. Dave was right—there was something going on, but it had nothing to do with them.

"Is there anything else?" He really wanted to get the hell off the phone.

"No." Dewey held on, but Chase ended the call, standing and stretching his arms over his head. He sighed and stretched again before returning to his email. He reviewed it and sent it to Dewey before closing his laptop.

"Done for the day?" Antonello asked as he stepped inside.

"Yeah. Thank God. I'm tired, and my boss can wear me out faster than anyone I ever met."

"The guy is a dick," Antonello said. "Why would I rearrange production schedules and impact dozens of clients all because he wants something a little faster? The arrogance." He put his hands on his hips. "Is that an American thing?"

"It's a Dewey thing. And yes, it's an American thing to a degree. Everyone likes to think that they're more important, and they press and push to see just how important they are. It's like Ricky. I set boundaries, and he pushes against them sometimes. We are taught to do that, and in business, it's something we do all the damned time to get an edge or make ourselves look good."

"It's not how we do business here."

"I know that," Chase agreed. "And he'll accept that the time frame can't change, but he'll bluster and growl a little in order to try to make himself look good. I pretty much ignore it." His phone chimed with a message, and he checked it.

"The dick?" Antonello asked, and Chase chuckled as he shook his head.

"Bianca asking what time I expect to be home." He sighed, remembering that he needed to speak with her about how long he expected to stay. Chase hoped they could work out an arrangement so she could look after Ricky for the rest of his time here. Another message came in asking if it was okay to make Ricky some dinner. Chase messaged that it was, realizing how late it had gotten. He needed to get going. "I'll see you this weekend," he said softly.

Antonello nodded. "We can meet and review the timeline again on Monday so you can tell your boss. I doubt there is any room, but we will see." He lingered for a few seconds, his gaze holding Chase spellbound for no reason other than the fact that he could.

"THANK YOU, Bianca," Chase said an hour later as he saw her to the door. They had negotiated a deal where she would look after Ricky while he was at work for the rest of their stay. She seemed pleased, and Chase was happy. He was pretty sure Ricky would be too. "I'll see you in the morning."

"Ciao, Mr. Chase," she said and closed the door after she left.

Ricky was already in his pajamas, and Chase read him a story and tucked him into bed before poking around the tiny kitchen area for something to eat. He found nothing and was about to run out to the restaurant next door to get something to go when a knock sounded on the door.

He wondered if Bianca had forgotten something and opened the door to Antonello with a bag in hand. "I bet you forgot to go to the market," Antonello told him.

"How did you know?" Chase stepped back.

"You've been working late." He stepped inside. "Isabella made some things for us, and I figured your cupboards would be bare."

"They definitely are." Chase cleared the small table of papers and set them aside as Antonello pulled a container of wide pasta with a thick meaty sauce out of the bag, along with bread, cheese, and a bottle of wine. Chase got glasses and plates, and they sat down to a delectable feast for the senses. "Oh God," Chase moaned around the first bite.

Antonello smiled and popped the cork on the bottle before pouring glasses for each of them. "I thought you would like it."

"Didn't you have plans? What about your parents? The family—won't they miss you?"

Antonello sniffed the wine and then sipped. "They have friends for dinner tonight, so I'm on my own. I could have joined them, but I don't want my mother and the other women to decide whose daughter to try to fix me up with next." He smiled. "I'm a coward, but I refuse to date someone and get her hopes up when I have no intention of going forward. I won't do that to anyone."

Chase swallowed his sip of the amazingly light and fruity wine. It was smooth and crisp. "You can't avoid it forever."

Those incredibly deep brown eyes met Chase's gaze, and he set down his glass. "I won't lie or hurt someone like that. Not again. I want to be happy, and I deserve that. Saddling some girl with a man who…." Chase could hear the words catch in his throat. "My family will be so upset when they find out. I don't know what my father will do, but my mother will go into full mourning like I died or something. Sometimes I swear she could out-drama a drag queen." He grinned.

Chase snickered. "Remember our trip to New York when we took you to the drag club?"

"How could I forget it?" He sipped some wine with a huge smile. "I both loved and hated it. I loved the entertainment, though, and had a great time once I let go of my worry." He set down his glass and picked up his fork. "I was so concerned that you or Elaine would think I was gay, and if you found out, then you might tell someone and it would somehow get back to my family." Sweat broke out on his forehead. "Hell, I'm still scared. I had a great time once the lights went down and I could just enjoy myself. But…."

Chase leaned forward, lightly touching Antonello's hand. "No one is going to tell anyone."

"Are you kidding? Ricky picked up on it. You heard him say something about kissing when we were at the Duomo. I know he's a kid and people don't pay attention to them, but… I don't know what I'm going to do. My family is the very definition of traditional. They could never imagine me coming out. To them it would bring an end to my family and everything generations of Gloriosos have built."

"It won't. People are more open now, and regardless of their religion or history, your family will love you."

Antonello snorted. "You haven't met my mother. She's a real ballbuster. My father is a quiet, thinking man who is more practical, but having a gay son is going to stretch him to the very limit."

"So what do you do? Get married like your mom wants? Hide for the rest of your life? Spend it alone? Who the fuck wants that? You don't deserve it, and if your parents expect you to live a half life because of something so… inconsequential, then what the hell is wrong with them? Your parents don't want a son, they want a robot… unthinking, unfeeling, just following the programming of someone else." He shook his head. "And for the record, I don't want that for you. I want you to be happy, to be able to be yourself—the smiling, fun guy I knew in college. The one who was whip-smart, intelligent, serious, and yet managed to steal the flag from the rival team at homecoming and flew it outside the stadium bathroom." He smiled, that memory one of his favorites. He still had no idea how Antonello pulled it off. "That's the guy I want you to be, and you can't be him if you spend all your effort keeping a big part of yourself secret and locked up from the rest of the world. And now that I've shot off my mouth and told you what I think, I'll shut up. And no… I would never say anything to anyone." He held Antonello's gaze, his fork dangling off his fingers.

"I wish things were different. I do. But I have a duty to the family, and I have to be the one to carry our legacy forward. There is no one else capable."

"That gives you authority. Your father and mother are not going to walk away from you. Will they be upset, surprised, disappointed, and maybe a little crushed? Sure. They saw a future for you that won't come to be. I know my mother felt that way. She got over it. Of course Elaine having Ricky helped a hell of a lot."

Chase could see the indecision in Antonello's eyes. "I just don't know."

"You don't need to go home in an 'I'm gay' T-shirt waving a rainbow flag tonight. This isn't something to do on the spur of the moment. Think about it and give yourself a little breathing space. But for God's sake, be true to the man you are, not the one they want you to be." Chase picked up his glass and downed the last of the wine before refilling it. "I know that being someone else is wearing, and doing it for years will only sap all your energy."

Antonello sighed loudly. "What can I do?"

"Maybe talk to a close friend. Tell them… her." He held Antonello's gaze. "If you ask me, I think your friend Isabella has already figured it out." He continued eating the amazing dinner. "And let me tell you, anyone who can make food like this is very much in tune with their feelings and those of others. This Isabella cooks with her soul, which tells me she understands hers and each person's that she cooks for." He cleaned his plate and sat back. "I've done way too much talking." A hell of a lot more than he ever intended.

"I guess I have a lot to think about," Antonello said.

"Yeah. But don't think too hard. You don't want smoke to start coming out of your ears. That would be bad."

"Who has ear smoke? I wanna see it," Ricky said as he came out in his pajamas, rubbing his eyes.

"What are you doing up?" Chase tugged Ricky onto his lap. "You should be in bed, asleep."

"I woke up hungry and heard you talking," Ricky said softly. "My tummy wants two cookies."

"We don't have any cookies." He handed Ricky a piece of the bread. "You can eat this. It has butter and a little garlic. It's good." Chase held Ricky as he ate the bread and drank some water, then cuddled close to him. "I'll be right back." He took Ricky to his small bedroom and tucked him into bed again. He rolled right over, holding his stuffy. "Sleep well." He turned out the light and left the room, then pulled the door mostly closed.

Antonello stood at the end of the short hall, his glass in hand, watching him. "I'm jealous of you."

"Why?" Chase asked.

"Because of Ricky. Because I will never have a son of my own. And maybe because I gave up on my chance for one—on my one chance at real happiness." He downed the rest of his wine and set his glass aside, taking two quick strides, eating up the distance between them.

To say that Chase was surprised was an understatement, but as soon as Antonello's hands touched his cheeks, sliding gently before drawing him closer, Chase stilled, wondering what was next.

Antonello drew even closer but hesitated for a fraction of a second before kissing him. And again Chase didn't move. It took him a few seconds to realize what was happening before he responded, returning the heated kiss with one of his own. He closed his arms around the man he had longed to kiss since college, pouring years of pent-up want and frustration into it.

Antonello pressed him back until Chase bumped the wall before pulling away.

"We have to be quiet." The last thing Chase wanted was for Ricky to see him and Antonello like this. It was enough that he joked about them kissing, but Ricky did not need to see it, or the fact that his pants were way too damned tight.

"I don't know if I can do that," Antonello whispered. "But I'll try." He pulled Chase away from the wall and propelled him a few steps to the next door. He opened it, pressed Chase inside, and closed the bedroom door behind him. This was no slow, gentle seduction, but years of denied desire flooding to the surface in a wave that drew Chase along, seemingly out of control. And he did nothing at all to stop it.

He pulled his shirt over his head and let it fall to the floor before working the buttons of Antonello's white shirt, his hands shaking enough he was tempted to rip the fucking thing off him. Their kissing grew more heated as soon as they were skin to skin, and Chase wanted more. It seemed Antonello felt the same way, because he pressed Chase down onto the mattress. Heat built between them as Antonello slid his leg between Chase's denim-covered ones, their hips coming together.

"Fuck," Chase breathed as he ran his hands down Antonello's back and over his tight, hard ass. Jesus God! Somehow he managed to slide his hands around and unfasten Antonello's pants. But was able to do little else as they each held the other so tightly. It was enough, and Chase slipped his hands under the fabric, gripping Antonello's bare ass, earning a deep groan that they cut off with another kiss that left Chase's head spinning and every inch of him on fire.

Somehow he shimmied Antonello's pants down. He kicked them off, and Chase frantically got his own off and onto the floor with a little help from Antonello.

A noise caught Chase's attention, and he stilled, the two of them watching each other in the moonlight that spilled through the window. There was no additional sound, so Chase tugged Antonello down into an intense kiss that left them both panting.

Skin to skin, heat to heat, they moved against each other. Chase shut his eyes, closing off his sense of sight to more fully hear the way Antonello breathed and the way the breeze filled the room, feel the way he held Antonello against him, the slight roughness of his chest hair against Chase's skin. He wanted to experience it all, remember it all, especially every time he inhaled… surrounded by Antonello's intense scent that rocketed him onto cloud nine.

"I need you. It's been so long since I let anyone close," Chase whispered as he splayed his hands against Antonello's back, wanting to feel everything all at once.

"Do you have protection?" Antonello asked.

Chase shook his head, chuckling softly. "I didn't think something like this was going to happen, and I wouldn't even know how to go into a store and ask where the condoms were." He smiled and loved Antonello's soft one in return.

"I suppose you're right."

Chase held his cheeks, keeping Antonello's gaze locked on his. "There's nothing to worry about." He rocked his hips, pressing up against Antonello, loving the way his eyes widened and his breathing hitched. Rocking them together, Antonello quickly got the picture, and together they moved their hips, cocks sliding past each other, pressure and friction building between them. That was enough, more than enough, and Chase guided Antonello until both of them quivered. Chase's hands shook, and he knew he wasn't going to last. "That's it, let it go."

Antonello blinked, body filled with tension. "Don't want this to end."

"Doesn't have to. We have all night," Chase whispered, and Antonello nodded, both of them holding on to the edge of a knife until they tumbled over together. Chase swallowed the groan that threatened, holding Antonello as his release barreled into him. Being silent only added to the moment, enhancing the pleasure.

Antonello held him closer as the energy slipped from both of them. Chase wrapped his arms around Antonello's back, closing his eyes and letting himself relax and enjoy the moment. This was that quiet time when the world seemed to halt, if only for a few minutes, when everything was perfect and the worries and cares of the outside world were forgotten. "God," Chase whispered.

"I know." Antonello settled next to him, and Chase slipped out of bed and returned with a towel. After a quick cleanup, he added the towel to the clothes that littered the floor and settled next to Antonello, sliding his fingers through the hair on his chest. "What do we do now?"

"We rest a little."

"I believe someone promised that we had all night," Antonello teased.

"We do. Now close your eyes and relax. We're safe here. Both of us are." Chase nestled closer. "This is just the two of us, you and me." Chase was glad his normally swirling thoughts were still and quiet. Thank goodness. All he wanted was to enjoy this moment. The million questions could come later.

Chapter 10

THE ROOM was quiet, almost silent, with just the soft sounds of the sleeping city, when Antonello woke. He quietly slipped out of the bed and searched the floor for his clothes. He needed to get dressed and out of here before a number of things happened. First, he didn't want Ricky to find him sleeping with his daddy. That would be bad and lead to questions that he figured neither of them wanted to answer. Secondly, he had to sneak into the family home and get up to his room before his parents woke and realized he wasn't there. The last thing he wanted was for his mother to convene the Spanish Inquisition.

In the living room, he finished dressing and quietly left the room, heading down to the lobby and out into the night.

The city was asleep and yet not. The lights on the Duomo shone, and downtown glittered, even if there were few people out to see it. He walked the quiet streets, passing around the cathedral to the side street. He turned a few corners and slipped into the side entrance to the family palazzo, going through the kitchen and up the back stairs to his floor, where he slipped into his room, undressed, and fell into his own bed. Thank God that had worked.

"SO WHERE were you last night?" his mother asked as she came into the breakfast room. "I know you were out late and got in early this morning." She sat down and was brought a plate.

Antonello could never put one over on her. "Are you and Papa going to the Duomo for Mass?" He decided to ignore her questions altogether and only speak about things he wanted to talk about.

"You didn't answer my question."

Antonello shrugged, and thankfully his father came in to breakfast. "I got a call from America on Friday. It seems they want things faster."

"What did you tell them?" Antonello ate some bread with Parma ham and sipped his juice.

"That if you made the schedule, then that was the end of it. But I think it isn't over for him." He sat down at the table, and a plate was brought for him.

"There is nothing we can do. Our schedules are set, and they agreed to them. I have their signatures." He waited while his father read the paper the way he always had for as long as Antonello could remember. "I'm not worried about it."

"What if they back out?" his father asked.

"Then they have to pay all costs associated with the setup as well as forfeit all deposits already paid. I made sure that we would come out ahead regardless of what they did." He wasn't stupid, and he wasn't going to do business at the whims of a dick. "We will meet all our commitments as promised, so there is nothing to worry about." Antonello returned to his breakfast.

His father nodded.

"Father, I know what I'm doing. My friend—"

"The American?" his father said in English.

Antonello continued in Italian. "He and I went to college together. I know him. He is a good person. His boss is not. Chase and I are working well together, so no one is going to back away. We delivered the first stage early, so Dewey was trying to push things up. He did not get what he wanted because there is no room in the schedule." He ate his breakfast, trying to act as though this was just business. Just talking about Chase made his heart beat a little faster, and if he wasn't careful, his mother would pick up on it.

"This is the same man you have been seen with all over Florence?" his mother asked as though she were planning something. "He is an old friend of yours?"

"Si," Antonello answered. He finished up his meal before excusing himself. Sunday morning breakfasts were something to be endured under his mother's ever-watchful, ever-planning gaze. Now his parents would go to church, and he could get a few hours of rest and quiet.

"The priest remarked last week that he hasn't seen you in quite some time," his mother said, changing forms of attack to one even older than her attempts to find him a wife. Ever since he'd returned from college, he hadn't attended Sunday Mass except on a few holidays because it made his parents happy. His mother hinted and tried to press him to go at least every month. It was a battle of wills that he had no intention of losing.

Antonello knew that as soon as he gave in to the force of nature that was Contessina Glorioso, all his defenses would crumble and that would be the end of his independence.

"Give him my best," Antonello said as he left the room. He went to his rooms and closed the door, making sure he was alone. He sat in his chair, wondering about Chase and wishing he had been able to stay.

I'm sorry I had to go, he texted Chase, holding his phone as he waited for a reply. But he didn't get one.

A knock on the door startled him out of his intense screen watching. He opened it, and his mother breezed into the room, ready for church.

"What is it?" Antonello asked.

"We must talk." She seemed earnest and agitated. "You hate me telling you this, but you must get married."

"In my own time," he told her.

She shook her head. "Your father is getting older, and he is slowing down. I see this. So do you. You must be ready to take over everything, and you must get married and have a son so there is an heir." She looked almost frantic, which was so not his mother. She was always composed and calm. "You know this is the future the family must have."

"What has changed?" Antonello asked. "Why this push right now?"

His mother's eyes grew laser focused. "Your cousin Lorenzo," she began.

"The womanizing idiot who picks up tourists and takes them to the family store? He is a menace." Chase needed to find a way to remove him from the family line of succession altogether, for the sake of everyone.

"He is going to be a father," his mother said, dropping a bombshell that stole Antonello's next comment right off his tongue.

"Cosa?"

"Aria is pregnant. And if she has a boy…." She stared at him.

"It doesn't change anything," Antonello said, but he knew that wasn't true. It didn't matter that his cousin had the morals of a rabbit and the business acumen of a badger. If he had a son, Antonello's father would feel obligated to let Lorenzo return to the firm, which would be a disaster. Getting rid of him the first time had been costly enough, but a second time would be impossible. As long as he had a son, however, Lorenzo would be able to hold the future of the family and the business over all their heads.

Antonello's mother quirked her lips, seeing through him instantly. "You must do something. Come to church with your father and me. You can pray to the blessed mother to help you find a wife." She reached for his hand, and he took a single step back.

"I think Mary has many other more important things to do than to find me a wife. You go and say a prayer for me. I have work to do, because whether Lorenzo has a child or not, someone has to see to it that the business continues. And Lord knows if Lorenzo gets involved again, we are going to need all the preparation we can get." He turned away and pulled out fresh clothes from his closet.

"Antonello," she snapped, using the same tone she had when he was a child.

He paused. "Mother. I'm fine. You go to Mass with Father. I need to think."

"You could think in church," she added, but he shook his head. Finally his mother left the room, and not long after, his parents went out for Sunday Mass. Antonello sat in his chair wondering what the hell he was going to do.

A MESSAGE CAME through from Chase almost an hour later. It seemed he and Ricky were out and he hadn't realized his phone wasn't charged. *My mind was elsewhere last night, and I think my brains got a little scrambled.*

I've already dealt with my mother… twice. Talk about getting brain muddle.

I get it. Ricky and I are going out for a walk, but maybe I'll see you later. He's fascinated by the Ponte Vecchio and wants to see it again. Chase sent a smiley face, and Antonello hurried to his closet to change into clothes suitable for being seen around town on a Sunday, then headed out to the bridge.

It wasn't hard to spot Chase. He and Ricky were in the very center, watching the water as it passed underneath. "Mr. Nello." Ricky spotted him first and ran over. "Papa says that there's a secret passage."

"There is. It's right up there." Antonello pointed above them. "It's closed right now because they are working on it. The passage is really long, and it goes from the Palazzo Vecchio over there…." He lifted Ricky so he could see better over the balustrade and pointed to the tower. "It passes the Uffizi, and then over the bridge here and to the palace over there."

"That's the Pity Palace. Daddy and I went there."

"It's actually the Pitti Palace. It sounds just a little different." Ricky nodded. "I understand you're learning Italian."

"Bianca taught me. See. 'Ciao, bello. Dov'è il bagno?'" he added with a grin. It was always good to be able to ask for a bathroom.

"Those are good. Do you know more?"

Ricky nodded and began speaking full sentences. The syntax was a little off, but Ricky told him about seeing the Duomo and walking over the Ponte Vecchio. Then he seemed to go off script and put together his own thoughts, which were jumbled, but it was a valiant effort.

Chase came up next to them as Antonello gently corrected Ricky and had him repeat the phrases correctly. Geez, he was smart and soaking things up fast.

"Apparently he and Bianca speak in Italian now, at least most of the time." Chase lightly bumped Antonello's shoulder, and he set Ricky on his feet. Ricky hurried to the other side of the bridge, and they followed. "Coming here was the best thing for him. He's learning a second language and is being exposed to so many different things."

Antonello nodded. "I'm sorry about this morning. I woke up and didn't want him to find us. I had to sneak back into the house because I didn't want to face my mother's questions." He rested his hands on the railing, watching the water as it flowed beneath them. "My cousin's wife is pregnant."

"The one we met here on the bridge with some other woman?" Chase asked, shaking his head.

"Yes. Aria is pregnant, and my mother shared the news as though it were the coming of the apocalypse. Of course she's using it to add pressure for me to find someone and get married." Maybe coming here was a mistake. Chase hadn't asked him, and he'd just barged into their day. With the way he felt right now, he was not going to be adding any fun or joy to the day.

"And are you?" Chase asked.

"I don't know what I'm going to do. Maybe it's time I just told my parents the way things are. They will explode with drama, but then it will be over and I can deal with the fallout."

"You have to do what you're comfortable with," Chase said.

Antonello had expected him to press him to open up, but no. He truly seemed to understand and was backing Antonello. He almost didn't know how to take it.

"I wish I knew a way forward for you, but I don't."

"I know. This is my own problem." There was no easy answer. His duty to his family told him one thing, and yet that was not at all in line with parts of who he was. Up until now he had hidden the part of himself that didn't fit, but that became more difficult each day. Something was going to break, and the longer it went on, the more he was convinced that it was going to be him.

"Maybe. But there are times when we all need someone to talk to."

"Daddy, can we go now?" Ricky pointed toward the city side of the bridge.

Chase scooped him up. "Let me guess. You saw the gelato shop and want some?" He swung Ricky in the air to giggles of delight. "We can get you some, but we need to go farther away from here." He strode toward the city, with Antonello next to him. They passed a store selling *pietra dura* items, and Ricky asked to stop so he could look at the pictures.

"Gramma would like one," Ricky said.

"We already got something for her," Chase told him.

Ricky pooched out his lower lip. "But they're pretty."

"I know, but we don't need one right now. Maybe later, okay?" Chase distracted him with tickles and got Ricky out of the store and down the street past the way overpriced gelato shops. One thing was a truism in Florence: the prices got higher the closer you were to the Ponte Vecchio. At least in general. That was part of the reason their shop was so successful. His father had long ago decided that the family would sell their goods at the same price at all their stores in the city, regardless of location.

"But I want gelato," Ricky said as he came to a stop.

"There's lots of places." Chase took Ricky's hand and led him around toward the Duomo and back to where Antonello had taken them a few days ago. "See?"

Ricky picked out his flavor while Antonello sat at one of the tables on the sidewalk, waiting for them to get what they wanted.

"We got you one," Ricky cried as he handed Antonello a chocolate pistachio cone. "Daddy said you would like this." He sat down, and Chase gave Ricky his cone before joining them.

"I swear I'm going to balloon up the longer I stay here. It's almost like being on holiday all the time. There's always excitement, and the city seems like a party every day."

"You get used to it. After years of that sort of energy, you learn to ignore it, because you have to. Every day can't be a holiday, as you put it, because work needs to be done. And after a while, it just gets exhausting. I walk by the Duomo every day, and on Sundays my parents attend Mass there. It's our family church. To the tourists, it's an architectural wonder, but to us, it's something more personal. So many of the things the tourists flock to are just part of our everyday lives. My family makes part of our living by tourists crossing the Ponte Vecchio, but for the rest of the city, it's a bridge to get us from one side to the other." He shrugged.

"You really love this place," Chase said.

"I do. It's fun," Ricky interjected. "There are all kinds of fun things to see, but too many naked people." He stuck his tongue out, and both Antonello and Chase chuckled.

"I like it too, and I've seen those naked people since I was younger than you." Antonello smiled, and his gaze shifted to Chase.

"Daddy, you look gooey," Ricky said, his head turned from side to side like he was watching tennis. "Mr. Nello too."

Chase tickled him, and Antonello pulled his gaze away. He needed to be careful. If a six-year-old could sense how he was feeling and the way he looked at Chase, then others could as well.

Ricky yawned, and Chase reminded him to eat more and talk a little less. "You need to finish before it melts, and then we should go home. It's been a busy week for all of us. We have some movies, and a little quiet time will be good."

"But I want to see Santo and Gerardo." Ricky smacked his lips after the last of his gelato.

"I'll let Isabella know, and we can arrange for you to play with the boys again," Antonello said.

"But for now, we need to go home. We've had a big day. There will be plenty of time for you to play with the boys, and we're going to be here in Florence long enough for you to see everything." Chase grinned. "You know, we're going to be here long enough that we could take a weekend trip to Rome."

Antonello smiled. "It's only two hours by train, and my family has a small villa in the city. If you want, we could go in a few weeks. The initial testing should be complete, and we'll be between tasks until the limited production run. Everything is on track." He smiled brightly.

"What about your parents? Will they use the house in Rome?"

"No. The only one who has recently is my cousin." Antonello looked upward and groaned. "He and his wife like to go there for weekends."

"And they won't be there?"

Antonello smirked. "I know how to make sure they aren't. Leave that to me. I'll get the tickets, and we'll go to Rome in a little under three weeks." Time couldn't go by fast enough for him.

Chapter 11

"THERE HAS been a supply problem, but Glorioso resolved it this morning," Chase told Dewey, adding the resolution before the guy could blow up again. He was getting tired of this, and the tension with his boss had him jumping every time the phone rang. The past three weeks had been nothing but stress, with the summer's humid heat translating into the project.

"You didn't tell me about this," Dewey challenged.

"Yes, I did. I had it on my weekly update for the past two weeks as a possible threat to the timeline. That threat has been removed. A supply has been found, and what we needed will be here in plenty of time. Testing and verification on this end are nearly complete, and I got a signoff from our team yesterday." Everything was truly going well. The only real trouble was Dewey's management by chaos. "The next run of product using the exact method for production will be made on time. That way product assembly and testing can begin." Chase checked the clock and groaned. He needed to get out of the office soon.

Dewey went quiet, and Chase wondered what he was thinking. "All right. It looks like everything is set. Make sure it stays that way." What a jerk. Even when things were going right, he found a way to look on the dark side.

"That's my job," Chase said, trying to keep the snark out of his voice. "It's getting late here."

"Yes. It probably is. Have a good weekend, and I'll talk to you Monday."

Chase cleared his throat. "I'm off on Monday."

Dewey made some sort of sound and then said goodbye and hung up.

Chase shook his head as he stared into the phone before shoving it into his pocket. He had already packed his things, so he hurried out of the office. Antonello's office was empty and had been for most of the past two weeks. He had business in Milan, so they hadn't seen each other in a while. It was strange how quickly Antonello had slipped back into his life… and how much he missed him. Chase wondered if Elaine would be angry with him. She had been so hurt when Antonello left after college. More than once, he wondered if he was doing the right thing.

His phone rang as he left the building and strode through the streets toward the center. "Hey, Mom." He hoisted his bag to his shoulder as he spoke.

"Don't 'Hey, Mom' me," she snapped.

Chase groaned. "What is it?" He kept moving because he needed to get Ricky so they could make their train in little more than an hour.

"I Facetimed with my grandson, and he told me that you are dating someone. A Mr. Nello." Her voice had that same tone she used when he was in *so much* trouble. "Chase Wilson Anderson, what do you think you're doing?"

"Excuse me?" he snapped back, pausing at a street corner at the edge of the pedestrian zone.

"It's bad enough that you have to work with this man, but he hurt your twin sister… and you." She sniffed and then blew her nose.

Chase groaned. "I work with him, and Antonello isn't the same person he was then. Neither am I, for that matter." There had been so much water under the bridge since then. But he would be lying if he said that he hadn't wondered if Antonello was going to hurt him again.

"What does that have to do with the price of peas?" Mom really had herself under a head of steam.

"Mom. Elaine was my twin and my best friend. You know that. She was a kind person who threw herself into life—all of it. And yeah, Antonello hurt both of us, and I don't know how Elaine would react to seeing Antonello again, but I do know that she had a huge heart and that maybe she'd forgive him. I see some of the same person I knew in college… while at the same time, someone with a sense of duty and what's right that wasn't there back then." It was so hard to explain it to her. "He's been good to us, and Ricky really likes him. And you know that he's a better judge of character than either of us."

His mother sniffled again. "I know. But all I remember is your sister crying in my arms after he left, and…. It's hard for me to think of anything else. And I miss you and Ricky. It's going to be months before I see him again…."

"I know. But think of the things your grandson is seeing and experiencing."

His mother groaned. "Tell me about it. He spoke to me in Italian for the first two minutes of the call." Now she seemed to brighten. "He seems to love this nanny you have for him, and tells me that they only speak Italian."

"Yeah, Mom. That was Bianca and Ricky's idea. I had nothing to do with it." He was so proud of his son. "Mom, I have to get home. I love you, and I'll give Ricky a hug from you." He hurried through the streets, passing throngs of tourists heading in every direction.

"Okay. Love you too." She hung up, and Chase picked up his pace. He reached his building and hurried up to their new quarters. It had taken them less than an hour to move from the residence hotel to a small two-bedroom furnished apartment less than a block away. They had a little more space, and it felt more permanent than a hotel. Ricky stood as soon as he came inside, dressed and ready, with his dinosaur suitcase right next to him. Bianca stood, and he thanked her for watching Ricky and for being willing to continue watching Ricky.

"Everything is ready for your trip," she said gently, kissing Ricky on the forehead. She smiled at both of them and left in an equal hurry. Chase hoped she had fun weekend plans too.

"Let's go," Ricky said.

"I need to change my clothes, and then we can go." He hurried to his room to the sound of Ricky's sighs. "Christ on the cross didn't sigh so loud."

"Huh?" Ricky asked as Chase closed his door. He undressed and put on comfortable clothes and good walking shoes. Then he grabbed the bag he'd packed that morning and found Ricky in the same place.

"Andiamo," Ricky cried. He hurried to the door, and they left. Chase held one of Ricky's hands, and Ricky pulled his bag over the cobbles with the other. One good thing about being here: they had both gotten used to a great deal of walking.

Antonello waited for them just inside the station, and he led them to the track and onto the train. "I was starting to get worried."

"Dewey called." Chase figured that was all he had to say. He didn't want to start the weekend talking about him.

"Where do we sit?" Ricky asked as Chase turned toward the back of the train.

"Where are you going?" Antonello asked as he headed forward. "We're this way. I booked us business-class passage." He led them through a door into a car with plush seats around nice tables. "We have this entire area."

"Can I sit by the window?" Ricky asked. Chase nodded and let Ricky get into his seat while he stowed the bags and sat down himself. "How fast does the train go?"

"Really fast. It's one hundred sixty miles to Rome, and it will take an hour and a half. So the train goes about a hundred miles an hour." As Antonello explained, they began to move. It was barely perceptible, except for the station passing outside, and soon they were speeding through the Tuscan countryside, smooth as glass even though at times they were moving nearly 280 kilometers an hour.

When Ricky started to fidget, Chase got out his activity bag with coloring book and crayons. Then he sat back, relaxed and content. "This is nice."

"It is." Chase agreed. He was tempted to close his eyes, except he didn't want to miss anything.

"What do you want to see in Rome?" Antonello asked.

Chase shrugged. He hadn't given it much thought. "Things that we can do outside. I don't think Ricky is up for museums and stuff like that."

"There's lots to do."

"No naked people with bare penises," Ricky declared before scrunching his face. "And no boobs." He didn't even look up. The people in the seats across the aisle from them did, with snickery smiles. Chase rolled his eyes, and Antonello smiled.

"There's a pool at the villa, so you can go swimming," Antonello told Ricky, which got a real smile.

"If that's the case, we may never leave the villa," Chase said, ruffling his son's hair.

Antonello leaned over the table. "You say that like it's a bad thing." His eyes grew deep and his voice rough. Chase's throat ached, and he was glad for the table or else he'd have made quite a spectacle of himself.

"I wanna see things… after swimming…."

Antonello smiled. "Like what?"

"Bianca said to see the Trevi Fountain and the Coliseum, and the building with a hole in the roof." He rattled off the highlights. "And I want gelato."

Chase tickled his son. "Of course you do." He looked over at Antonello for guidance.

"The oculus at the Pantheon," he supplied, and Chase nodded.

"Go back to your coloring. We have a little while yet." The truth was the journey was passing quickly, and ten minutes later, they began slowing before pulling into the station on time. Chase put Ricky's things away and got their bags while Antonello got his and held Ricky's hand. Ricky chattered away about almost everything as they exited the station and got into a taxi.

"What's that?" became his favorite question as they rode through the city.

"That's the Coliseum," Chase said reverently as they passed the ancient stadium. Chase ran out of answers, but Antonello didn't, explaining about Trajan's column and the arches of the ancient ruins before they left the city center behind, ending up in a quieter area on a ridge with an amazing view of the rest of Rome.

"We're here," Antonello said, and Chase got out, admiring the manicured grounds and the palazzo that graced it.

"Let me get this straight. You have this and you just use it on weekends?"

"My great-grandmother on my father's side lived here in Rome, and she left it to my father when she passed away. He prefers to live in Florence, so it isn't used as much as it should be. I telephoned ahead to make sure everything was opened up and ready for us." He strode toward the front door like the princeling he was and went inside.

"You have to promise me that you won't touch anything. Okay?" All Chase could think about was Ricky breaking some priceless Etruscan vase or something.

"What are you waiting for?" Antonello called. "Come on in."

He held the door, and they went inside. Cool air surrounded them as they entered a foyer with a small fountain and pond in the middle, the water bubbling away. Antonello led them up a marble staircase and down a hall.

"Is this my room?" Ricky asked as he stepped into every child's fantasy. The walls were frescoed with dancing and jugging animals.

"Was this for you?" Chase asked.

"These are three hundred years old. They were done for children who grew up long ago." He lifted Ricky and spun him around. "And yes, you get to sleep in here." He put him back on his feet. "Your daddy and I will be sleeping at the end of the hall." Once again those eyes grew dark, drawing Chase in, making him forget everything but Antonello and the way he felt next to him on crisp sheets.

Ricky climbed onto the bed, grinning. "When do we eat?"

"The kitchen is stocked, so why don't you put on your bathing suits? The pool is out back, and I'll meet you there with dinner." He carried out the bags, and Chase got out Ricky's suit before leaving him to change.

"Antonello," he said softly, and he appeared in the doorway straight ahead.

"I have you in here." He tilted his head to the next door, and Chase went inside. Antonello closed his door before opening the one connecting the two. "I hope this is okay."

"It's lovely." He set his bag on the bed he had no intention of using. "But I need to get my suit on, and you do too, because Ricky is going to be down here as soon as he's ready."

"Daddy!" Ricky called.

"See?" He kissed Antonello and closed the connecting door, because if they got changed together, it was likely that Ricky would never get to swim at all.

"YOU TWO go in the pool," Antonello said as he stood to the side in his square-cut bathing suit. "I'll be right back." He went inside, and Chase got in, the salt water embracing him.

"Is it cold?" Ricky asked with water wings on his arms.

"No. It's really nice." He smiled as Ricky jumped in the water. He came up grinning before swimming away like the fishy he was. He went to the other end before coming back, kicking hard to propel himself through the water.

He came right up to Chase, and Chase lifted him out of the water. "Catch me?" he asked, climbing out of the pool. Chase held up his arms, and Ricky jumped. He caught his son to laughter and plenty of splashes.

"I brought something to eat and drink when you're ready," Antonello said as he set a tray on the table. Then he tugged off his shirt, giving Chase a great view, then dove into the pool, making almost no splash. He surfaced right near them, giving Ricky a little splash and getting one in return.

Ricky swam away.

"He's a little fish, I swear, and he has no fear of the water." Sometimes Chase wished Ricky wasn't so bold. But then his eagerness also meant he didn't have to worry about getting him to take swimming lessons. He wanted to learn.

"Are there pool toys?" Ricky asked.

"I don't know, but when we go back into the city, we can find some." Antonello stretched at the edge of the pool, the water coming just above his waist. Damn, he was more handsome now than he had been back in college, and that was saying something.

"Mr. Nello, come swim with me."

Antonello glided away from the wall like he was born for the water. He lifted Ricky right out, then splashed him back in. Ricky came up laughing, and soon the game evolved around how far Antonello could lift him. After a while, Antonello got out of the water, and Chase joined him at the table. Antonello poured glasses of wine and set out plates of cheese, meats, bread, and olives.

"Isn't he hungry?"

Chase shook his head. "He won't eat until I make him get out of the pool. I swear he'd live in there if I let him." He got the towel he'd brought out for Ricky. "Come out and get something to eat. You can go in again afterwards."

"But Daddy, I'm not hungry." Ricky got out of the pool, dripping water.

Chase wrapped him in a towel. "You can be not hungry and go back in the pool after you eat." That sounded kind of crazy even to him, but Ricky didn't question it and climbed onto one of the chairs. Chase handed him a piece of cheese, and he gobbled it down, then wanted more, so Chase made him up a plate, and Ricky settled in to eat.

"I thought you were having a stroke or something. You were talking gibberish."

Chase sighed as he sat back in the plush chair. "Raising children will do that to you."

IT TOOK another hour before Chase made a pruny Ricky get out of the pool for the night and into his pajamas. It was still warm, so they sat outside with Ricky on Chase's lap, quickly falling asleep. Chase sipped from a glass of prosecco. "It sure is lovely here, and so quiet. You'd hardly know we're in Rome."

"Yes. This property has been in parts of my family for a long time. The frescoes in Ricky's room were painted for a lucky child in the eighteenth century. Other parts of the villa date to the seventeenth century, but they are hard to spot because it has been renovated a number of times."

"So much history and so many things that have to be cared for and maintained."

"That's it exactly. This villa will come to me along with everything else. But I'll own none of it. I'll be little more than a caretaker for the next generation, and they will be the same. My father started the metallurgical business as an offshoot of the jewelry we've made for years, and that has done very well."

"Is that your father's?" Chase asked. "I mean, does it belong to the family, or is it his to do what he wants with? Maybe I'm being kind of dumb, but I don't know how things like this work. There is no generational wealth for us."

"I suppose that technically, everything is my father's. He inherited it and owns it… for the family. And since he built the metallurgy business himself, I suppose that would be his to do with as he wished." He shook his head. "Things don't work that way. Dad's talents are at the disposal of the family." Antonello seemed to run out of words. "Let's put it this way: once I inherit it, then it will be part of the legacy that I need to protect."

Chase got up and laid Ricky on a lounge chair, glad he had changed into dry clothes. He stood behind Antonello and ran his hands down his chest. "That sounds like a lot of expectations."

"And those are just the beginning. It all will rest on my shoulders." He tensed, and Chase gently massaged the muscles. Chase was just starting to understand what the duty to Antonello's family meant, and to Chase's surprise, he found he wanted to help, but he had no idea how.

"I need to get Ricky to bed, but I'll be back in a few minutes." He positioned Ricky at his shoulder before taking him inside and up to the second floor. Ricky easily went into the bed, barely waking before going right back to sleep. Chase sat with Ricky for a few minutes to make sure he was truly settled before turning out the light and quietly leaving the room.

He descended the stairs slowly and exited the back of the villa, coming to a stop at the far edge of the terrace and looking down at the softly lit pool. Antonello swam fully submerged, his sun-kissed body sleek as he glided unbroken under the water. Chase swallowed hard as the long line of tanned skin passed in front of him. He stopped and realized what he was seeing before taking the first steps down toward the deep blue pool, his heart pounding a mile a minute.

Chapter 12

ANTONELLO REACHED the edge of the pool and poked his head up to see where Chase was, finding him standing at the edge, looking down at him. "Come on in," he said softly, standing so the water rested at his waist. He knew damned well how clear the water was and that Chase knew he had discarded his suit.

"You're…."

"I know. There is no one else here, and Ricky's room is on the other side of the villa." He extended his hand, holding it in place as Chase tugged off his shirt and dropped his pants before stepping out of them and lowering himself into the water.

Antonello waited until Chase took his hand again before tugging him to him, their bodies coming together easily. Chase sighed as Antonello took him in his arms, sliding a hand down his back to cup his smooth butt. "This feels so naughty."

Antonello smiled. "Nope. This is private. Ricky is asleep, and this is an opportunity for us to have a little adult time." He closed the distance between them, kissing Chase gently but deeply, loving the taste of him.

Chase pushed back harder, pressing Antonello toward the side of the pool, shaking as he went.

"It's okay," Antonello said, "È l'attesa." Chase paused, then seemed to understand. "Abbiamo tutta la notte." He kept his voice low, drawing them closer. "There is no rush."

"I love it when you speak Italian," Chase whispered. "There's something sexy about it."

Antonello nuzzled the base of Chase's neck. "Amore, non c'è fretta."

Chase groaned as he ran his lips over his skin, stretching to give him access. Antonello stroked Chase's chest, letting his fingers bump over a nipple, each movement slow and languid, even as his heart pounded. "Come with me," he whispered and then slowly fell back into the water, drawing Chase with him.

He swam, the soft water sliding across his skin, stoking his excitement. Chase swam more slowly, and Antonello slid right next to him, running his hand over Chase's back as he glided. When they came up for air, Chase's eyes were dark, almost mysterious as he stood on the bottom of the shallower section, his cock just peeking out of the water. "You're driving me crazy."

Antonello drew closer. "We could go upstairs."

Chase backed up against the side of the pool, and Antonello closed the distance between them. When Chase leaned against the tile, Antonello slid under the water, slipping under his legs before rising. Chase's knees ended up on his shoulders, and Antonello leaned forward, kissing him hard before backing away. He slipped his hand around Chase's cock, pointing it at the sky before sliding his lips around it, taking him deep, to a groan that echoed off the water.

"Jesus," Chase whimpered as Antonello swallowed him. His experience was limited, but he wanted to make this good for both of them. After everything that had happened and all the water under their bridge, he felt that this was where they were supposed to be. He had been such a fool years ago. "Tio," Chase said, and he stopped. He hadn't heard that nickname in so many years. It had been what Chase and Elaine had called him in college, and he'd honestly never thought he would hear it again.

He pulled away, holding Chase right there. Damn, this was a sight: Chase laid out under him, stretched beautifully with everything possible ahead of them. "Say that again." He took Chase deeply once more.

"Tio," Chase whispered, and Antonello damn near swallowed his cock. Chase held tightly to the side of the pool, and when Antonello felt his hold fading, he straightened up, letting Chase's cock slip from his lips and his legs slide down into the water. "Jesus," Chase sighed.

Antonello lifted him up onto the side of the pool, spreading his legs. Chase leaned back, and Antonello sucked him even harder, loving the way Chase came unglued under him. He adored the way Chase seemed to let go with complete abandon. And he wanted more, letting his hands wander over Chase's belly and chest, lightly pinching his nipples, his cock jumping each time.

"I don't…," Chase gasped, and Antonello backed away. He was not ready for things to be over, and Chase's quickening breath told him he was approaching the edge. "Jesus." He lay back, stretching out on the pool deck.

Antonello slipped under the water to cool himself down and then climbed out of the pool and grabbed a towel for each of them. He dried his hair before helping Chase to his feet. "Come on. There's a nice soft bed waiting for us, and we can make love for as long as we have the energy." He wrapped the towel around his waist, and once Chase had done the same, he took his hand and led him inside.

"DADDY!" RICKY shrieked at some point in the night. Chase sat straight up with Antonello right behind him. Chase jumped out of bed, pulled on a pair of shorts he'd brought in just in case, and hurried out of the room. "Daddy!"

"I'm here," Chase said calmly. Antonello got out of bed, dressed, and made his way down the hall. "There's nothing to be scared of." Chase rocked Ricky as he held him.

"I woked up and didn't know where I was and…." Ricky sniffled, and Chase turned on the light.

"Do you remember now? You're in the room with all the animals."

Ricky sniffled. "But what if they come to life when it's dark?"

Antonello smiled. "I used to wonder the same thing," he said gently from the doorway. "This was where I slept whenever I visited when I was your age. I used to wonder if the animals would come to life, and I tried to stay up to see. But they never did. I didn't get to meet the juggling bear or the acrobatic racoon. They stayed on the walls because they're just pictures." He came closer as Ricky watched him. "I used to dream that they were my friends, but I never got to play with them."

"Oh. So they were nice? Not like the bad man?"

"We ran into a pickpocket in Florence when we first got here," Chase said softly. "He didn't get anything, and I thought Ricky might have forgotten about him."

Antonello nodded his understanding. "They aren't at all like the bad man. They smile and laugh and play, just like you do. No biting or growling allowed. I promise." He ruffled Ricky's hair. "Are you ready to go back to sleep?"

"No," Ricky said with a yawn. Chase rolled his eyes and settled Ricky back in bed.

"Here's your stuffy. He'll protect you always." Chase seemed to know exactly what to do. "Now close your eyes and go back to sleep. I'm still here, and I'll protect you from bad men. I promise." He leaned over Ricky, kissing him on the forehead, and then quietly left the room. Ricky seemed settled, and Chase padded back to their room. "He should sleep now."

"Has he mentioned anything about this man that you saw?"

"No, but sometimes you never know. He may seem to forget and then he'll bring things up weeks later. I suspect it's because he's in a strange place and woke and got scared. It happens." Chase settled in bed, and Antonello did the same, sliding an arm over his chest.

"It's safe here."

"Yeah?"

Antonello hummed. "I didn't turn on the alarms in the house itself, but the ones on the edges of the property are all on and watching. So relax and go to sleep. We're all safe, and there is nothing to worry about." He closed his eyes, loving Chase's warmth as the night breeze cooled the room.

"CAN WE swim again?" Ricky asked at the breakfast table outside near the pool. He looked at the water like it was the most enticing thing in the world.

"Maybe later. But how about we go into Rome to see all the really good stuff? I can tell you stories," Antonello offered. "And yes, we can get gelato." He was starting to really get to know this kid. Heck, in a lot of ways, he was just like him. Antonello remembered getting gelato with his dad any number of times. "Okay?"

Ricky ate and nodded. Chase seemed a little dazed, and Antonello wondered if Chase had gotten enough sleep. "You okay?"

"Yes." Chase smiled. "I'm fine." He sighed and finished his juice before getting up. "Let's get ready to have some fun."

"But remember, no naked people," Ricky warned.

Antonello lifted the kid out of his chair. "I can't promise that. This is Rome, and there are statues of naked people everywhere. But you don't have to look at them, okay? Just put your hands over your eyes, like this." He demonstrated. "And your daddy and I will tell you when it's gone." He grinned and set Ricky down. "Now let's go." He led them outside and to a waiting car that drove them to the center of the city.

Antonello explained about the Coliseum and what happened there. He also told stories about the other ancient ruins and had the driver get them close to the Pantheon. Ricky was fascinated by the oculus, standing in the middle of what had been the largest dome in the world for a thousand years until the Florence Cathedral was built.

"Daddy, there really is a hole. Why?"

"So that the roof would weigh less and so they could let light inside," Chase said. "This was built a really long time ago."

"Is it older than you?" Ricky asked.

Chase ticked him, his laughter echoing off the ancient walls. "Yes. It's lots older than me. It's even older than Grandma."

Ricky's mouth fell open, like that was a seemingly unfathomable amount of time. They stayed as long as Ricky wanted to look, then left.

They spent the day seeing the Trevi Fountain as well as the Fountain of the Four Rivers in Piazza Navona. They ate wonderful food and had plenty of gelato, got T-shirts, and basically had an amazing day. After dinner, they rode back to the villa, with Ricky falling asleep in the car seat almost as soon as they pulled away from the Piazza Venezia.

"Thank you. I'm not sure how much Ricky is going to remember, but I know I'm never going to forget this." Chase closed his eyes as the driver wove through the city traffic until they reached the outskirts and pulled into the villa driveway. Antonello wasn't sure if Chase would take Ricky right up to bed, but as soon as they pulled to a stop, Ricky's eyes slid open and he peered out the windows.

"Can we go swimming now?" The kid had a one-track mind.

"THIS HAS been great," Chase said as he stretched the following morning. The house was still quiet, and Ricky had slept through the night after an hour of swimming and a day full of activity. "I'm sort of sad to have to go back." He rolled over with a smile. "It seems kind of dumb to say that, since we're returning to Florence, not some hick town in Idaho." Antonello loved that smile. "But this has been so much fun."

"It has." He reached for his phone, pleased to find no messages or emails that required his attention. Everything he had could wait until tomorrow. "I like Rome, but Florence is more…."

"Even with the tourists, it's quieter," Chase said softly.

"Yes," he agreed and stretched himself. "I'm willing to bet that Ricky is going to be awake at any moment and that he is going to be hungry." He got out of bed and bent over to pull on a pair of shorts.

Chase tugged him back into the bed, holding him tightly. "I locked the door after checking on Ricky."

Antonello chuckled softly. "I see." He kissed him, feeling happier than he had in a very long time. The cares and weight of responsibility felt light at the moment. It was like they mattered less with Chase around… like he could handle them better. Maybe it was just his imagination, or maybe he just missed what Chase seemed to offer him: a kind of acceptance and care that had nothing to do with the family he'd been born into or the responsibility that carried.

"Daddy," Ricky called from outside, "where are you?"

Chase groaned, but Antonello kissed him and patted his cheek. "It's okay. Go see to him, and I'll be down in a few minutes to get us something to eat. We slept in, and we need to leave for the station in a few hours."

"Can I go swimming? I got my suit on already."

Antonello sprawled back in bed as Chase went through the connecting door and closed it after him. He smiled, listening as Chase's laughter drifted into the room, followed by giggles from Ricky.

"Ask Mr. Nello, okay?" Ricky pleaded, and Antonello could almost see that pooched-out lower lip and Chase trying to figure a way to say no, but knowing he'd cave.

"We need to have breakfast first, and then we can go swimming for a few minutes before we leave for the train."

Antonello got out of bed, dressed, and cleaned up quickly before finding the housekeeper to let her know that they wanted to eat out by the pool. "Breakfast will be ready soon," he told them, and Chase took Ricky's hand and led him out back to the table next to the sparkling water. Ricky looked at it like the pool had sirens calling him.

"Grazie," Antonello told Rachel as she brought their breakfast to the table and then left them alone once more. She worked for the service that cared for the villa, and he'd arranged for her to be there so they could be sure to depart on time.

"Can I swim now?"

"Go ahead. But you have to eat something when you get out," Chase told him. Ricky pulled on his water wings and jumped right in. "Stay on this side of the pool."

"I will, Daddy," Ricky called back as Antonello poured juice and got a plate with some bread, cheese, and prosciutto, along with some lovely fruit.

"What will happen when we leave here? Do they close the place up?" Chase asked.

"No. The service will clean up and make sure the villa is secure. They are very trustworthy and will come in every few days and make sure things are okay."

"Daddy, can we come back here again?" Ricky asked after getting out of the water, dripping all over the pool deck.

"Maybe," Antonello told him.

"Yeah. Now go swim, because you have only five more minutes. And then you need to eat and get dressed so we can get on the train." Ricky ate a piece of cheese before jumping back in the water.

"You're really good with him," Antonello said.

"How were your parents growing up?" Chase asked.

"I had a nanny who looked after me. I spent much more time with her than I did with my parents. They were always busy, but I saw them in the evenings at dinner. I was given the pasta course to tell them about my day. Even now, the sight of fish makes me talk faster. Dad was good and we did things together, but my mother… she was the tough nut. I don't think she liked being a parent—at least not until I was twelve, and then I was sent to boarding school in Bologna. It was a lonely way to grow up sometimes, but my nanny was good to me, and she made sure I got the attention I needed."

"Do you still see her?"

Antonello nodded. "You met Maria before. My first nanny, the one I had until I was eight, is in Naples now with her family. I see her whenever I'm there on business." He couldn't help chuckling. "She still makes me her amaretto cookies every time I tell her I'm coming."

Chase watched Ricky play. "Jump in one more time, and then you need to get out and towel off." Ricky did as he was asked, and then Chase wrapped him in a towel and got him settled with some food and a small glass of juice.

They talked through the rest of breakfast. Chase got Ricky dressed before packing up. Antonello ordered a car, and they met it in the drive. They piled in and rode to the main train station, where Antonello got Ricky a gelato before they boarded the train back home.

Part of him was ready to return, but another part, the one that was truly relaxed and happy, wished they could stay in Rome forever.

THE RIDE back was comfortable. Once they got off the train, they walked through to the historic center of the city. Antonello escorted Chase and Ricky home, sharing a kiss with Chase once Ricky had hurried to his room.

"I'll see you tomorrow."

"I wish you could stay," Chase whispered.

"Me too. But I better go. I have things I need to do before I go into the office, and I suspect Ricky is going to conk out at any time. I'll see you in the office." They kissed again, and Antonello left through the front door, walking the streets he knew like the back of his hand to his family home. He went inside, carrying his case, only to be met by his mother, her expression thunderous.

Chapter 13

CHASE DRAGGED himself into the office on Tuesday. Antonello's door was closed, which indicated he wasn't in yet, and that was unusual. Antonello usually beat him into the office. Chase checked the time and sat down at the desk, where he pulled out his laptop and checked emails. Thankfully there were only a few automated reports from the weekend, which he scanned and cleared before getting a start on the week's tasks.

His job was to see to it that everything went according to schedule and to keep everyone working together and management up to date. On the surface it didn't seem like much, but it meant he spent a lot of time writing emails in an attempt to try to stave off questions and phone calls, or worse, meetings that wasted everyone's time. Dave ran most project meetings, with Chase reporting progress on his pieces of the larger project, and he wanted to be ready.

He was just finishing some materials for Dave when Antonello thundered into the office. Chase heard the receptionist greet him, and Antonello ground out a good morning before stomping into his office, closing the door harder than he needed to.

Chase opened their connecting door and poked his head in. "Who pissed in your Cheerios?"

Antonello responded with a spate of Italian that Chase did not need translated to know that something was very wrong and that it had to do with his mother. "She met me when I got home, demanding to know what I was doing in Rome. Apparently she had invited the daughter of one of her charity acquaintances for lunch on Sunday, and I wasn't there."

Chase shook his head. "Didn't you tell her you were in Rome?"

Antonello shook his head. "My father knew, but…." He sighed. "I don't feel the need to tell my mother where I am and what I'm doing. I have my own wing of the house, and I come and go as I please."

He glowered at Chase. "I basically run the entire family business, and I don't need to inform my mother about every move I make."

"Okay." Chase stepped back. There was definitely more to this than Antonello was saying, and he wasn't going to pry, but he figured his mother's matchmaking was beginning to drive a real wedge between them.

"She wanted to know why I brought you and Ricky to Rome."

This could be interesting. "And what did you tell her?" Damn, sometimes he was just wicked.

"That you were a business associate and I took you to Rome to show you around. Which was true."

Chase nodded and stepped closer, then shut the door. "And us only using one bed—was that business?" Chase had been teasing, but Antonello clearly didn't take it that way. He turned to Chase in complete shock.

"You know it wasn't. My feelings for you personally have nothing to do with business. When we're here, we act professionally at all times, but when we're… when it's just us, then everything is different." He swallowed, and Chase wondered just how different Antonello felt. Weeks ago they had decided that they would be professional and nothing more. But that seemed to have flown out the window. Now Chase wasn't sure where things stood with Tio. Were they friends with benefits, or was something more happening? He had more than his own heart to think about. Ricky was becoming attached to Mr. Nello and asked about him all the time. If things went badly, then it would be more than just him who had the potential to get hurt.

"Duuuude…," Chase said, harkening back to their college days whenever he'd explain to Antonello that he was being played. He needed to get this conversation back onto more solid ground.

"Stronzo," Antonello swore without heat, his expression softening. "I have never taken business associates to Rome before, and I have certainly never…." Words seemed to have escaped him.

"Slipped anyone the big Italian sausage while you were there?" Chase teased.

Antonello glared at him before shaking his head. "You Americans."

"I seem to remember you have a thing for them, especially around the pool at night." He kept his voice low, and Antonello growled at him. Chase smiled and turned to leave his office. "I guess I should ask if things are okay now with your mother."

Antonello shrugged. "I have no idea. I told her again that she needed to back off and leave me alone, but somehow I doubt she will. My mother is on a mission, and I really have no idea how to get her to stop."

Chase knew a surefire way to get her to back off, but that would involve Antonello telling her the truth, and Chase wasn't sure that he was ready to do that. Maybe he never would be. It was difficult to see Antonello being pulled like this, but there was nothing he could do about it. This was a decision Antonello had to make for himself.

MAYBE THIS thing with Antonello was getting out of hand, and maybe he had let himself go too far down the rabbit hole. He really liked him—hell, he knew it was more than that, but he was afraid to use the word, even to himself. What surprised him most was how quickly his feelings developed and how easily he pushed everything else aside, including his concerns about the past. Maybe he needed to give himself a chance to think. The past weekend had been wonderful, and Chase had found that the more time he spent with Tio, the more his feelings grew and the more he liked being the center of his attention. It was like a damned drug. The problem was that he wasn't sure he was ready for Antonello rehab.

He absently checked his emails and forced his mind through his tasks at hand, picking up his phone when it rang late in the morning. "Morning, Dewey," he said when he saw the name. "What's up?"

"The verification here was completed over the weekend. I just sent Glorioso our signoff, and we have built a number of prototypes, and those are being tested in the lab now. We used the remainder of the pieces that were sent earlier."

"Okay. I'll speak to them about getting more shipped as soon as they are able." There was little else he could do. "I've also been going over the rest of the engineering specs, and I saw a few changes."

"Yeah. I had Dave make them. They're really small." Dewey seemed proud of himself. "I think we can incorporate them going forward."

"But they will mean redesigning the most important components, including the piece from Glorioso that you're just about to sign off on." Chase kept himself calm. Dewey thought he was a brilliant engineer, but he was sloppy and didn't look at the entire picture. All he wanted was fast, which didn't work in their business. The FDA and other agencies would see to that. "Also, if those changes are made, it will affect how the unit performs, and the FDA isn't likely to approve it." He was trying to politely explain that changes to design couldn't be made on the fly.

"I sent the same information to Dave, and he hasn't raised any issues," Dewey countered.

"Okay." Chase looked up as Antonello stuck his head into the office. Chase smiled and then rolled his eyes. "But unless you want to completely start over on this end, we can't make those changes. We'd have to go back to the drawing board and redo everything here, and any savings would be eaten up by the changes that would be made over here."

Dewey groaned. "Fine. Just ignore my suggestions. I'll let Dave know to disregard them. Stick with the design you have." Chase could tell that he was not happy, and he knew Dewey would somehow manage to get even with him. "I'll speak to you at the staff meeting tomorrow." Dewey hung up, and Chase met Antonello's gaze.

"Dodged a bullet with that one," Chase said.

"I figured. So everything is good?"

"Yes. Dewey is sending his approval, which should act as final signoff for the next phase." At least that step was behind them.

"Do you want to get lunch?"

Chase looked at his list of tasks that had just gotten longer, thanks to Dewey's meddling. "I don't think I can right now. I have more calls to make. But thank you." He wanted to get out of the office but didn't have the time.

Antonello closed the door, and Chase called Dave to touch base.

"Sometimes I don't know what he's thinking," Dave said once he pulled up what Dewey had sent. "That would require a whole new wave of FDA design approvals. Months of work…." All because he wanted to play design engineer all of a sudden. Chase was willing to bet that Dave was thinking the same thing he had been.

"I wanted to let you know."

"I'll handle it," Dave said firmly. "Don't worry about it at all. Speak of the devil. I need to take Dewey's call."

Chase ended the call and continued working, head down, until a knock on the door pulled his attention. Chase looked up to see Antonello with a plate of pasta, the scent filling the room, making Chase's stomach growl.

"Maria sent you something special," Antonello said, and Chase groaned as he took the first bite.

"She is a goddess." He smiled and swallowed. "Thank you for thinking of me."

Antonello closed the door and stepped closer to his desk. "I'm always thinking of you, during the day, at night… when I'm supposed to be in meetings…." He leaned closer. "You seem to occupy my thoughts all the time."

Chase met Antonello's heated gaze, speechless. "Tio…," he started softly. "I'm really not sure if this is such a good idea. We're working together, and…." He set down his fork. "You left after college because of your duty to your family. And as far as I can see, nothing has changed. I know you care for me, that is obvious, and I care for you, but the duty that is so ingrained in you, the one you put most everything in your life on hold for, is still there, and I don't want to be the one to get hurt." His chest ached just saying the words, but he had to. There was no other choice. "I'm here for a few more months, and then I'm supposed to go back to the US." He tried to keep his voice level.

Antonello nodded slowly. "Maybe you're right and this thing between us is some sort of fantasy, some holdover from our college days that was suppressed and is coming forward. But it feels right, and nothing has for me in a very long time. And I know you're here for a limited time, but I'd rather spend it with you and Ricky than apart. If you don't feel the same, then I'll understand. What I did back in college wasn't right, and I know I can't just turn my back on my family."

"I just don't see how this can go anywhere, no matter how much I might wish it could." The words felt like broken glass on his tongue. "Part of me says to walk away, and yet…." Damn, even saying the words was so fucking hard.

"Then don't." Antonello's eyes filled with hurt, and Chase could feel his resolve wavering. "I've been happier these past few weeks, with you, than I have in a long time, and I need some time to try to figure this out. My family is important to me, but…." He paused, and Chase held his breath. "So are you. And I know I can't keep living like this. I have to figure out a way to tell my parents who I really am."

Chase nodded slowly. "I understand. It wasn't easy to tell my parents, but I couldn't live a lie any longer. And if I'm being honest, I don't think you can either. I saw how free and happy you were this weekend."

"I was." Antonello shifted his weight from foot to foot. "My parents are so traditional and set in their ways."

Chase snickered. "There is at least one person who isn't. The one who had the vision to start a whole new division of the company business, the one who branched out and took a chance. I know a lot of us tell our mothers first, and I have never met your parents, but maybe you should have a talk, one on one, with your dad." God, he hoped to hell his logic was correct.

"I'll give it some thought," Antonello said, and Chase smiled. "Now I think we need to get back to work. I have a number of things I need to finish before I'm done for the day, and I bet you do too." He pulled open the door between their offices. "Enjoy your lunch."

Chase thanked him and went back to his tasks.

An hour later, well into the specs for another project that he was involved with, he picked up his phone when he got a text message. It was from Bianca, saying that Ricky wanted to know if it was possible to play with Santo and Gerardo. *He's been asking a lot.*

Chase answered that he would arrange it and that he'd take Ricky to Isabella's for dinner tonight. That should make Ricky happy, and it would mean that he didn't have to cook, which was always a good thing, especially after a full day of work.

I will tell him, Bianca messaged, and after a few minutes, he received a bunch of smiley-face emojis. Chase figured his answer had been the right one. He smiled and put his phone aside, then finished up his tasks before getting ready to leave.

"Hey, we're going to Isabella's for dinner. Ricky wants to play with the boys, so I'm going to take him over. Are you available to join us?"

"Let me check," Tio said, and after typing, he nodded. "I can. I have a dinner with my family tomorrow that I must attend. My mother is holding a fundraiser for the Uffizi. There are some pieces that are expected to come up onto the market soon that the museum is hoping to add to the collection. Apparently they were scattered from the museum at some point in the past, and Mother is determined to get them back for Florence." He continued typing for a minute and then closed his laptop and slid it into his Gucci bag. Then he left the office. "Do you want to meet at Isabella's in an hour?"

"Perfect."

"Good. I'll call her to let her know we're coming." Tio grinned. "Ciao." He strode down the hall and down the stairs to the first floor, with

Chase following his bouncing buttcheeks the entire way. Outside, they parted ways and Chase headed home, where he greeted Ricky at the door.

Ricky practically bounded into his arms. "Hey, buddy."

"I'm ready to go," Ricky said, holding up a fabric bag.

"What's that?"

"Legos. They don't have any, so I brought mine."

Chase loved that Ricky wanted to share. "How about you leave those here, and I'll talk to Miss Isabella about letting the boys come over? You can play Legos then." He could just imagine Lego obstacles spread all over the streets of Florence.

"But Daddy," Ricky said, complete with lip pooch.

"Don't try that. Now go get your shoes on," he instructed, and Ricky half sulked back to his room as Chase checked in with Bianca before she got ready to leave. She was a godsend, and he thanked her and paid her for the week. Then she left, and Chase quickly changed his clothes before getting Ricky and heading out.

The walk to the restaurant was wonderful, the cool night air, complete with a breeze, almost perfect. Ricky raced ahead as soon as the saw the restaurant. The boys met him, and soon they were off playing soccer down the cobbled pedestrian street while Chase sat at the table with Tio, who poured him a glass of wine.

"I see you started without me." He sat back, smiling as he sipped. "I'm really beginning to think of this place as home. It's familiar now, and I'm starting to make friends." He raised a glass as Isabella came out. He stood, and she greeted him with light kisses. He was about to ask her what magic she had in store for them when she stilled, staring. Then she whispered in Italian, and Tio turned, going white.

"Who is that?" Chase asked.

"My mother," Tio answered as a woman who seemed dressed more for a theater opening than dinner glided down the street toward them. She passed the kids, who stopped playing. Ricky ran over and stood next to Chase. She approached Tio but didn't take her gaze off Chase and Ricky.

"Antonello," she said gently, standing next to her son, "you need to introduce me."

He seemed shocked and didn't speak at first. "Mamma, this is Chase Anderson and his son, Ricky." She didn't extend her hand or even say anything, but her gaze went to him, then Antonello, and back to him and Ricky. He wondered what was going on behind her intense brown eyes, and he shivered slightly. Her lips pursed slightly, and then her expression reverted back, almost exactly as it had been, except for pure determination. Chase felt the blood drain from his head as fear settled in his gut. The old fight-or-flight response was so real, and all Chase wanted to do was grab Ricky and get the hell away from her.

Chapter 14

ANTONELLO'S MOTHER seemed to scan Chase and Ricky like her eyes were radar. Antonello was about to interrupt her when she snapped back to her usual cool aloofness. "I see." He wasn't sure what had put her off.

"Chase is the representative from Smithson," he said gently and then switched to Italian. "He is a business associate, and the contract he's working on is important to us. Remember?" He glared at her, wanting to snap at her about remembering her manners, but her lips turned upward.

"Of course. You're here for a few months. Are you enjoying our beautiful city?" she asked Chase in English. After a second or two, he nodded.

"Yes. I am. We are having a nice experience here."

Antonello noticed that Isabella was nowhere around, and even her boys were quiet and had moved near a corner of the restaurant, ready to disappear at any moment. Kids and dogs had good instincts, because his mother was formidable. He often wondered if she would make a good Disney villain.

"It was good to meet you," she said to Chase before turning slowly, almost like she was walking a runway, and then she glided off to the right, all eyes on her until she disappeared.

Chase held Ricky, his eyes huge.

"Daddy," Ricky said, squirming slightly before hurrying over to the other boys. In a few seconds, the game resumed, and their laughter dispelled some of the cloud still lingering from Antonello's mother's visit.

"What was that about?" Isabella asked quietly in Italian as she refilled wineglasses.

Antonello answered that he had no idea. He was still puzzling why his mother would decide to take this route to one of her civic meetings. Part of him wanted to think that she wanted to see him, but his mother was more interested in Chase and Ricky, which intrigued and worried him. Had he managed to give himself away and let his feelings for Chase show somehow? He had no idea how, but his mother had a better spy network than her distant Medici ancestors. Antonello never knew what to expect.

Isabella called to the boys that they had ten minutes and then returned inside. "What the heck? And I thought my mother could be frightening."

Antonello wished he had some insight. "That's just her." He shrugged, trying to let his own concerns wash off his back. His mother could suspect anything she liked, but he and Chase had done nothing wrong, and being seen together in public was not a crime and didn't mean anything. Still, the thought of his mother knowing how he felt about Chase didn't fill him with the dread he had always thought it would. In fact, maybe her knowing the truth would be a relief. "Though you never know sometimes," he added to himself.

Chase still seemed pale as he reached for his wineglass and downed half of it. "What if…?" He stopped himself.

Antonello shrugged. "If she knows, then I'll have to deal with it. But I'm going to be honest and tell her."

Chase seemed lost for a second, and then he nodded. "You think she figured things out about you?" he asked softly.

"We've been spending a lot of time together, and I stayed over in your rooms. Sometimes I never know what pieces of information she's going to gather. But if that's true…."

"How do you feel about it?" Chase asked quickly.

"I guess I'm okay with it. The truth had to come out one way or another, and all this hiding is wearing me out."

"Thank goodness," Isabella said as she placed a bowl of pasta on the table.

Antonello snapped his gaze up to her, and she rolled her eyes. "You knew?" he asked, switching to Italian because it was easier.

"Of course. I always watched the way you were good to women, but you never really showed any real interest. But as soon as Chase came to town, you watched him like a tiger, ready to jump to his defense at any moment. I think it's nice. You deserve to have someone in your life who excites you. Remember, you are Italian, and passion runs in our blood. Don't deny it. And you shouldn't let your mother and father keep you from pursuing it."

Antonello glanced at Chase, who watched the boys.

"See, I see you."

He swallowed a gulp of wine. "Did I treat women badly? Did I ever mistreat you?"

Isabella rolled her eyes. "You broke the heart of every woman who set her sights on you, but… meh… you never encouraged any of us either."

Then it hit what she was telling him. "*You?*" he asked. He loved Isabella like the sister he never had.

"Yes, at one time. But not anymore. You helped me through when I lost Luca, and I think I…." She turned away for a second. "It's better this way now. We are friends, and that's what we were always meant to be." She patted him on the shoulder before going inside and returning with a bowl of salad and a platter of fresh fish that looked amazing.

"You know that if I had ever chosen a woman, it would have been you." He flashed her his best smile.

She shook her head. "And Italian men are full of bullshit," she teased before calling the boys, who raced over. They all sat down, with Ricky sitting next to his dad, making yummy noises until he got to the fish.

"What's the rule?" Chase asked quietly and put a small piece of the fish on his plate. Ricky tasted it and then ate all of it and asked for more.

The tension Antonello's mother had spread earlier had mostly abated. But once Ricky was done eating, he climbed onto Chase's lap, and Chase held his son to him, eating less than he normally would. Antonello hoped Isabella didn't notice, but she seemed busy keeping her two boys from giggling and playing at the table.

Once the food was gone and Chase helped by carrying the dishes inside, Antonello said goodbye to Isabella with a kiss on each cheek, thanking her for an amazing meal. When he got back to the table, Chase asked quietly how he should pay her. "It doesn't seem fair that she should feed us like this," he said softly.

"Isabella and I have an arrangement. I eat here when I want, and she sends me a bill each month… and I pay her more than she bills. So please don't worry about it. Just enjoy the food. Besides, it's nice to see the three boys so happy." He decided to leave it at that. Ricky was waning and leaned against Chase when he returned to his seat to finish his wine. Antonello watched the two of them, jealous in a way that Chase had someone to love and who loved him no matter what. He sipped his wine, wishing once again that he had made different choices. Antonello kept telling himself that returning to Florence had been something he had to do, but that wasn't true. He had decided to come home and do what his family expected. It had been his decision, and in doing so, he had walked away from the two best friends he had ever. Antonello had no idea how different his life might have been if he had made a different choice.

Once dinner was over and they had drained two bottles of wine, Chase and Antonello said good night as the light began to fade. The boys had played for an hour longer, with Chase watching his son as though a huge bird was going to swoop down and grab him at any moment. "I need to get Ricky home and ready for bed." He thanked Isabella for her hospitality, and Ricky said goodbye, waving as Chase took his hand, and they walked down the street toward the Arno.

Antonello finished his wine before thanking Isabella for another amazing meal and then walked back to the family villa. He girded himself for whatever his mother had in store.

His mother and father came out of their sitting room as soon as they heard him close the door.

"You need to come in here," his father said in a measured tone that set his stomach churning. His mother was usually the one who led the sort of talk he was expecting, but his father…. This was worse than he thought.

He entered the room, finding his mother and father sitting rigidly on the sofa. "We need to talk. This is very important," his mother said. "I believe there is some information that you have neglected to tell us." She cocked her head slightly to the side.

Antonello nodded. "Yes, there probably is."

His father leaned forward. "Why didn't you tell us?" He sounded hurt, which was not the reaction he had expected from his traditional father, especially about this sort of thing.

"Because I didn't know how to. You and Mother are so traditional. I understand that I have a duty to the family, and I've always put that first… but I also deserve to be happy, and it's time I stopped hiding the person that I am."

His parents turned to one another and shared one of those silent conversations that came with being together for decades. "What are you talking about?"

Antonello paused, wondering what was going on. "The fact that I'm gay and that I have feelings for another man. That I will never marry a woman, and that no matter how many Mother tries to fix me up with, I will never fall in love with just the right girl."

There, he had said it. Whatever happened, he was now being honest with his parents, and if they turned their backs on him, then so be it. The family would find themselves in the hands of his cousin Lorenzo, and God help all of them.

His mother blinked as though she couldn't believe her ears, and his father almost seemed like he had been slapped. "My son is a *frocio*?" he said softly.

Antonello glared at his father. "Your son is gay, and I am still your son. Never use that word again." His father startled at his vehemence. "I will not be disrespected or spoken down to because of who I am. I've hidden a big part of myself from both of you because I was afraid of how you would feel, but I don't care any longer. You can think whatever you want, and you can cut me out of the family, but I will still be the same person, and I will not change to please either of you."

His mother's red lips parted and then closed again before she nodded slowly. "That explains a lot, but it changes nothing." Her glaze hardened, and she stood and left the room without another word.

"I never thought she would not know what to say," Antonello said as he turned to his father, ready for the onslaught.

"Being a member of this family comes with a price. I know it." His father put his hands in his lap. "Your mother and I were not each other's first choice. I was eighteen, and I fell in love with the daughter of one of the men who worked in the shop on the Ponte Vecchio. She had long black hair and eyes that sparkled like the stars. She also didn't stand for any of my attitude and gave as good as I did. Claudia and I were very evenly matched, but my father put his foot down and said that I was never to marry her. That she was not the kind of person that his son should be marrying. Then he spoke to her father and arranged for her to be sent away to school in France. I was never to see her again, and as long as I kept my promise, then Claudia would be able to pursue her dreams." His father sighed. "I let her go because we snuck into the Boboli gardens more than once, lying on the grass, looking up at the stars as we told each other our dreams. She wanted to be a doctor, and I didn't want to stand in her way." His father swallowed. "A year later, your grandmother and grandfather introduced me to your mother."

"You had to be very angry," Antonello said, and his father nodded slowly. "Why did you just give up?"

"Because I wanted what was best for her." He snorted, a sound Antonello had never heard his father make before. "That's bullshit. I didn't have the guts to stand up to them. I backed down and told myself that if she was happy, I could live with it. I went along with what they wanted, and I married the girl they wanted me to marry. I was lucky, because your mother is an amazing woman, and I grew to love her very quickly."

Antonello had never heard this story before, and he was intrigued. "Did you love her when you married her?"

"No," his father said honestly. "But that changed within the first year we were together. She shared my dreams and helped me lay the foundations for the expansion of the business. Your mother has never failed to support any decision I've made."

Antonello nodded. "But what does this have to do with me? I meant what I said. I will not marry a girl to please you, and I will not hurt someone that way." He leaned forward, drawing closer to his father. "And I will not allow my mother to canvass her friends to find out if they have gay sons. I will find my own partner." He knew his mother well. She might bluster and put up a fight, but once she accepted the situation, she would be back to trying to get him married, one way or another.

"Your mother and I only want you to be happy."

He met his father's steely gaze with one of his own. "And there is the issue. You think you know what would make me happy. You do not. In fact, you and Mother don't have a clue, because you do not know me. You only know the person I've allowed you to see. Like I said, I will choose my own mate." He turned to leave the room.

"Antonello," his father said as he reached the door. "I'm sure you will." He stood as well. "Now I need to see to your mother. There was something she wanted to discuss with us, but it seems that conversation will need to wait for now." He patted Antonello on the shoulder and left the room.

Antonello had no idea if what had just happened was good or bad. He was pretty sure he had his father's support, but his mother… well, that was another matter. He was tempted to go find her and get whatever she had in mind brought out into the open, but he didn't want to push.

Maybe it was best if he let his father talk to her first. His dad had a way of soothing his mother's nerves, and as long as his father accepted him, then his mother would eventually come to terms with the fact that he was gay. As much as she might try to push or prod him, she wouldn't go directly against his father.

Antonello poured himself a drink from the bar in the corner and went up to his room, where he sat at his desk and tried to get some work done, but he couldn't concentrate.

I told my mother and father about me, he said to Chase in a text.

That got an almost immediate answer. *Are you okay? Did they take it well? Do you need to come over here to get away from them?* Leave it to Chase to be supportive no matter what.

I'm fine. My mother walked out, but my father and I had a good talk. I think things between us are going to be okay.

I had that feeling, Chase sent, and Antonello found himself smiling.

You were right. Now I just have to deal with the fallout of whatever my mother decides that she thinks is in my best interest. He typed the words, hoping he got them right. *I'll have to wait and see how things shake out.*

It will be okay, and now you can be yourself. You don't need to hide any longer, and I hope you'll find that freeing. I did once I stopped trying to pretend and didn't worry about it all the time. He sent a smiley face, and Antonello sent one back. Whatever happened, he knew he could see it through. Still, Antonello didn't want to be alone, and right now he felt very much like he was flying solo.

Would it be okay if I came over later? He checked the clock.

Of course, Chase answered, and Antonello felt like maybe the quicksand under his feet had finally solidified.

Chapter 15

CHASE SET his phone aside, wondering what the hell was going on. He had been so sure that Antonello's mother had seen how much Ricky looked like her own son. But when Antonello messaged, it seemed that he had come out to his parents, so maybe that hadn't been it at all. This entire situation was becoming more confusing and unsettling by the day, and it was all his fault. He had decided early on to keep Ricky and Antonello apart and that his stay in Florence was supposed to be business and nothing more. Hell, the idea was that he'd stay angry with Antonello for what he'd done to Elaine, but that hadn't happened. None of the things he had told himself in the beginning had come to fruition. God, everything was a mess, and his life would be so much easier if he had just done what he'd said he was going to do in the fucking first place.

At least Ricky wasn't awake to see him pacing while he had his mini breakdown.

A knock on the door pulled him out of his thoughts. His heart raced a little faster as he went down and let him inside. "I didn't want to sit in my rooms alone."

Chase was shocked. "What? You told your parents that you were gay, and they just left you? They didn't stay to talk or to make sure that you were all right?" He snapped his jaw closed.

"My mother simply left the room, but my father and I talked." Antonello stood still, wringing his hands. "I have no idea what the real fallout is going to be. My father seemed to understand, which I have to say you were right about. My mother…. I have no idea. All she said was that me being gay explained a lot but changed nothing, and then she left the room." He looked pale, and Chase took his hand and led him to the sofa. Once he sat, Chase got him some water and settled next to him.

"Your mother already knew on some level, whether she wanted to admit it or not, and I'm willing to bet that she will come around." He wanted that for Antonello. Chase could only imagine how difficult it would be when a parent refused to accept their child for who they were.

"Probably. But I'm afraid that once she does, she will try to fix me up with men that she feels are the right kind of people. I don't know." He drank some of the water. "That's the thing. I have no idea what my mother is thinking or how she'll truly react. It's like she's a time bomb out there just waiting to go off."

"Hey," Chase said softly. "Your dad understood, and that's saying something. You came out and told your family who you are. Opening yourself up to anyone is hard. And you did it." He couldn't help smiling a little. Chase knew how hard and how difficult something like that could be.

"I hope everything is going to be all right," Antonello said.

Chase shifted on the sofa. "Okay. Let's look at this straight on. What is the worst that could happen? Your mother decides that she isn't going to talk to you? That she'll keep trying to fix you up with women? Because that isn't going to get her anywhere. Word gets around, and that will dry up fast. Your dad accepted you, so he isn't going to turn his back…."

"Yeah. But you don't know my mother."

Chase snickered. "I got a pretty good picture of her today, but you're right, I don't know her. She is your mother, though." It was all he had. He really did think that in the end everything would be okay between Antonello and his parents. There might be some drama, but eventually things would work out. At least he hoped so, for Antonello's sake.

"Like I said, my mother can be the most difficult person to figure out." He drank some more water before setting the glass on a coaster on the side table. "Maybe I should just go home and see what's going on. Maybe my mother will decide to let me in on what she's thinking."

Chase lightly touched Antonello's chin. "You don't have to go anywhere."

Antonello nodded and drew him into a kiss that quickly grew ravenous as Antonello pressed Chase back against the cushions of the small sofa, kissing the breath out of Chase. Antonello seemed to need him badly, and Chase was more than willing to give whatever Antonello seemed so desperate to find.

"Come with me," Chase whispered, and once they got up, he turned out the lights, led Antonello to his bedroom, and closed the door behind them. "Now it's just us. The rest of the world is outside that door, and it can stay there." At least for now. They would need to face whatever was coming, but Chase was determined to be there for Antonello. Coming out was hard enough, but doing it like this with a parent who seemed cut off from their child was extra hard.

He drew Antonello into a kiss, wrapping him in his arms as passion built between them. Antonello was a bundle of energy, practically shaking in his arms as Chase undressed them both. He wasn't sure what Antonello wanted or if sex was a good idea at a time like this, but Antonello pressed him back on the bed, and heat built between them. "Tell me what you want. What's going on?" he breathed, before Antonello kissed away any remaining words.

With each passing second, Antonello became more desperate, his energy level almost frantic. Chase held him, letting him use up the adrenaline that had to be coursing through him. He knew that Antonello needed a release, some way to let go of the hurt and worry that had gripped him for so long. Chase knew what he had to be feeling and wanted to see him through it.

"I don't know what's going on," Antonello whispered.

"It's freedom," Chase told him. "It's letting go of the worry and fear and being yourself." He cupped Antonello's stubbled cheeks. "Just let it go and revel in it." He kissed him and tugged Antonello down, wrapping his legs around Antonello's waist. It was just the two of them, which was perfect.

Antonello's breathing filled the room. This was incredible, and the two of them reveled in a shared sense of joy. Chase was so happy and proud of Antonello for taking this step, it was almost like he had come out all over again. It was a sense of peace, and the joy almost demanded to be shouted from the rooftops. That, combined with the sheer ecstasy, sent Chase sailing. No one made him feel the way Antonello did. No matter their past, it was now, this moment, that mattered. The rest was memories of the past or dreams of what was to come, but holding Antonello, listening to his breathing, feeling the pulse on his neck, the scent of him as transportive as a field of roses—those were now, and sensations he wished to add to memory.

"Is this what you want?" Antonello whispered as he ran his fingers down Chase's thighs and over the curve of his ass.

"Yes," Chase whispered. "There are supplies in the bedside table." He waited as Antonello got him ready before leaning over him, his eyes shining as their bodies joined. Chase gasped and his eyes crossed at the intense burn and stretch, and then he moaned as he held on to Antonello, feeling their hearts beat as one.

"Am I hurting you?" Antonello asked softly. Chase shook his head, unable to speak, but he hoped his eyes showed everything. They seemed to as Tio moved slowly, deliberately, joining them in a cadence of passion that built with each passing second.

"More. I'm not made of glass," Chase whispered into the humid air of his closed room.

"That I know. You're strong and smart, and I love watching you." He held Chase's gaze. "Your eyes shine with excitement, and I could bask in their reflected light for the rest of my life."

Chase stopped moving as he took in what Antonello said. Then he let the words wash over and past him. Things said in the heat of passion were often exaggerated, and Chase decided to take the words as a kindness rather than with a deeper meaning he was sure Tio didn't intend, no matter how wonderful they were to hear. Instead of dwelling on the words, he kissed him, sending them both into a deep well of desire that Chase hoped neither of them were able to climb out of for a very long time.

And damn, Tio had patience, rocketing Chase to the precipice of passion only to pull back before he reached the top, then drive him upward once more. Time and time again, Antonello took him on a wild, breathless ride until, together, they flew into the clouds, floating on an epic release that Chase hoped would never end.

MORNING CAME way too soon, and the last thing Chase wanted to think about was the fact that he had a meeting with Dewey first thing East Coast US time. What he wanted to do was call in sick and then stay in bed with Tio, whose head rested against his arm. He hadn't left in the night. Chase smiled and checked the clock beside the bed. It was a little before six, and he didn't have to get up for another hour. Chase closed his eyes once more and tugged Tio closer to him, holding him tightly. He sighed softly, a sense of contentment sinking deep into him. This felt right, and that both comforted and frightened him. It was so easy to feel safe and cared for with Tio right next to him, but it scared him too. Chase didn't live here, and eventually he would go home. There was also the lingering question about Ricky's parentage. Was Tio really Ricky's father? He had lived under the impression that it had been Elaine's boyfriend at the time of her death—the possibility of Antonello being

Ricky's biological father had never occurred to him until he got here. Maybe he had been deluding himself, thinking that no one else seemed to notice. Why in the hell did his life have to be so complicated and filled with mines he couldn't seem to avoid? It wasn't like he knew for sure, but some part of him still felt like he was lying.

"You're awake," Tio said very softly.

"It's still early. Go back to sleep," Chase said as a cool morning breeze freshened the air. He didn't want this to end.

"Are you sure?"

"Yes. It's really early, and there's no need for us to move. Not just yet." He felt like they were playing the scene from Romeo and Juliet where they teased each other about what time it was just to avoid ending their magical night together. Tio hummed softly and shifted closer. "I know we need to get up and go to the office, but we have time, and Ricky isn't going to be up for a while yet." He closed his eyes, hoping to fall back to sleep, but that didn't happen. Chase didn't want to miss a single second of their time together.

Tio pulled the covers up over both of them, the chill morning air cooling their skin. "I don't want to go, but I should get home so I can dress for work." Still, Tio snuggled down against him. "But I don't want to."

"Are you worried about your parents?"

Tio sighed. "I have no idea what I'm worrying about. Business associates are not going to care if I'm gay or not. All they want is to ensure that we deliver on time with a product they can count on. The rest is pretty much crap, as you used to say. As long as my father backs me, then it will not be an issue." He held Chase tighter, their warmth nicely melded. "I guess I don't know how to act. I feel different, and yet the same."

Chase drew Tio's gaze. "The important thing is to act the same, because you are the same person you were yesterday and the day before. The only thing that's different is that you are being honest about it. Nothing else has changed. You're the same man you were and will always be. You're confident, smart, and caring. You were always those things, just like you can be a hardnosed jackass. It's all part of the package that is Tio. And none of that has to do with the fact that you're in my bed rather than one of the women your mother tries to set you up with."

Tio chuckled. "I do have to say that if I were inclined that way, my mother tends to have good taste, but I think I would reject anyone she suggested on principle. I'll select my own partner, and I told my father that."

Chase chuckled. "Did he say 'father knows best'?"

"In his own way, I think he did. He told me that they only wanted the best for me. I told him that I would be the judge of that. I don't know if that will sway him and Mother, but I think the fact that I threw my mother off her game stands in my favor."

"But will she be angry?" Chase asked.

Tio let out a deep breath. "I don't really care at this point. This is my life, and I'm the one who has to live it. She needs to get it through her head that it isn't the sixteenth century and I get to make my own decisions. Besides, what are they going to do? Put my cousin in charge of the business? Though I suspect my cousin will see it as an opening once he hears. That man is so stupid." Tio pushed back the covers and sat on the side of the bed. "As much as I wish it were Saturday and I could stay in bed with you for hours, I have to get home so I can get ready for work. And you have things you need to do as well, including seeing to Ricky." Tio turned around and kissed him hard, threatening to ignite the heat banked inside.

When he pulled away, Chase smiled, basking in the warmth from Tio's eyes. Then he stood and slowly began to dress. Chase watched every movement as Tio's pants slid upward, covering that perfect ass, and then as his shirt obliterated the glow of his chest. He lay back as Tio finished pulling on his shoes. "I'll see you at the office a little later this morning."

"I don't know how I'm going to be able to pretend that nothing has changed." Chase had already found it hard to act like he and Tio were simply colleagues, and after last night, it was going to be nearly impossible.

"Me neither, but we'll figure it out. We have jobs to do, and those have to continue. I can't get lost in thoughts about you all day, no matter how easy that may be." He smiled and kissed him once again before leaving the room.

Chase lay back, listening as the front door closed behind Tio. He knew he had time, but there was no way in hell he was going to fall back to sleep, so he got up, showered, and dressed before waking Ricky and making sure he was ready when Bianca arrived.

"Daddy," Ricky asked, wiping his eyes, "can we have pancakes?"

Chase checked the time and set about making his son breakfast as Bianca arrived. He gave each of them a plate, with Bianca looking at the flapjacks like they were alien food. Still, she took a bite and seemed to enjoy them.

"I have to go," he told Ricky, giving him a kiss on the head.

"Ciao, papà," Ricky said, waving, and Chase said goodbye too, then left and made his way to work.

CHASE WAS earlier than usual, and the building was mostly quiet. He went to the office he was using and got to work answering the emails that had come in after he'd left work the day before. There was nothing pressing, and he relaxed as he made up the list of things he needed to accomplish. Fortunately they were in a quiet time and Chase was able to take a breath and get his mind around the revelations of the previous day.

Tio came in just as he was finishing. He went right to his own office and closed the door. Chase kept his mind on his work and refused to read into Tio's behavior. They were at work, and professionalism needed to be the order of the day. Still, he hoped Tio was all right and that he hadn't had a run-in with his mother this early in the morning.

Some time later, Tio opened the door between their offices. "Everything is on schedule, and there are no issues."

"Great. I'll report back that we're still on schedule and check in with the team in the States as soon as they come in to verify there are no issues on their end." He loved it when things went according to plan, and a good part of his job was to ensure that they did. Chase smiled and then turned away because it was the only way he could stop himself from looking like a lovesick teenager. "Thanks." He began typing as Tio drew closer to his desk.

"You know, in Italy, we believe that business is personal and that we should get to know the people we are working with so that we can build trust. Business isn't sterile like in America. We don't cut ourselves off from it the way you do."

"Yeah, I've seen that. But you do realize that I have to live with my boss, who is a real dick." He swallowed hard. "And I'm starting to find it difficult to keep my perspective." It was his job to do what was in the best interest of his company, and that was becoming harder. He couldn't care less whether his boss was happy, because he was such a self-centered jerk. And the people above him, well, they let him get away with the crap he pulled.

"I see. Do you need me to back away?"

Chase paused. The thought sent a cold shiver up his spine. "No. Just understand that I might need some distance sometimes."

A knock sounded on Tio's office door. He excused himself and went through to his office. "Mamma," Tio said before continuing in Italian. Chase didn't understand the words, but the accusatory tone was unmistakable. He went to the door to close it, but Tio's mother strode into his office, turning her vehemence on him.

"What is she saying?" Chase asked, but Tio seemed completely shellshocked and didn't say anything. "I'm sorry, but I don't understand." He tried to keep his voice level, hoping a calmness he really didn't feel might deescalate whatever was going on.

"My mother is accusing you of stealing her grandson," Tio finally said before speaking to his mother. She yelled back, then reached into her pocket and pulled out a photograph. She shoved it at Tio, speaking fast, pointing to the image. "She says that your son—Ricky—looks exactly like I did at that age." He passed the picture over, and Chase gasped, because the image in the photograph looked so much like Ricky.

"I didn't know," Chase said.

Tio sank down into one of the office chairs. "Was Elaine pregnant when I left?" Tio asked. The gaze that had been so warm and soft a few minutes earlier was now as cold as stone.

"I don't know. She started dating someone else a while later and then told us she was pregnant. She said that he was the father, and I had no reason not to believe her." Chase could barely breathe. "He was never in the picture once she told him she was pregnant, and she had the baby with just me there. And when she died, Elaine left a will delivering Ricky into my care. I adopted him four years ago." Tio's mother spoke again, rapidly. "I know you speak English," Chase told her.

"If he is my grandson," she began, "then this adoption of yours can be overturned." She whirled around and stomped out of the office.

Chase watched her go.

"Did you know?" Tio asked. "I know what you told my mother, but…." He didn't move from the chair.

Chase shook his head.

"But you thought it was possible," Tio accused.

Chase paused and then nodded once. "Elaine's boyfriend was Spanish, and now that I think about it, he looked quite a bit like you. I think now that was why Elaine dated him. Maybe she was trying to replace you. I couldn't have guessed, and I still don't know." It was time for him to be as honest as he could. "After that day on the Ponte Vecchio, I never meant for you to see Ricky again. I was afraid that you would recognize yourself in him. But then no one made the connection, not you, Isabella, or the other people we met. No one even looked at Ricky twice, so I thought I had imagined it all."

"But Mother...."

"It seems she saw the resemblance almost instantly." Chase stood. "Look, I don't want to cause trouble, but I'm not going to give Ricky up. He's Elaine's son, and I adopted him, so I'm Ricky's daddy now." Maybe it would be best if they simply left Florence and went home. He'd think of something to tell his boss, and then he could get the hell out of Dodge.

"It's not that simple." Tio lifted his gaze. "I have a duty to my family, and if Ricky is my son, then he stands in line to inherit everything—all of this. That is how things work in my family. I would have an heir, a legacy to pass everything down to. There would be no worry about my cousin trying to wheedle his way into the business. Do you understand?"

Chase understood all too well. "Yes, I do. This duty that you have— it's the same one that you had when you left after college, the one you had when you abandoned Elaine and me. And it's the same duty that, if you happen to be Ricky's father, drove you to leave him and his mother behind. So excuse me if I tell you that I don't give a damn about your family duty, or honor, or any of that crap, for that matter. All I care about is my son, and I will do whatever I have to in order to keep him safe." Chase went to the desk and snapped his laptop closed. He put it in his bag along with the picture of Ricky he had placed on the desk. Then he headed for the door.

"Where are you going?"

Chase didn't answer or pause on the way out. No matter what Smithson said, it was fucking time he went home. This family duty shit of Tio's had messed up his life before, and he'd be damned if he was going to allow it to pull his life apart again.

Chapter 16

Leave it to his mother to drop a bombshell and exit dramatically.

The door had barely closed behind Chase before Antonello slumped in his office chair, wondering what the hell had just happened. His mother had said that Ricky was his child. He had to admit that Ricky looked a lot like the photo of him that his mother had thrust under his nose. It was hard to get his head around it. Him, a father? Shit, what was he going to do? Was it true? He had no idea, and he tried to breathe and clear his mind, but all he could think about was the possibility that he had a son. And what was he going to do if he did? He had no answers to any of those questions, but if he wanted some, he wasn't going to get them sitting here.

He jumped to his feet and hurried toward the exit.

"Sir, you have a meeting in half an hour," the receptionist said as he passed the desk.

"Reschedule it," he answered without pausing as he ran for the door. He raced outside and down the cobbled streets toward where Chase and Ricky were living. He knocked on the door as soon as he arrived.

What the hell had he been expecting? It was likely Chase wasn't going to let him in.

"Mr. Nello," Ricky said with a grin as he opened the door, with a young woman behind him.

"Is your daddy here?" he asked as Chase approached carrying his bag, his expression as serious as a heart attack.

"Daddy?" Ricky raced out past Antonello to greet him.

"You and I have to talk," Antonello said seriously. "Now."

"I can take Ricky to the park," the woman said, with Chase hesitating before agreeing.

"Keep a close eye on him and be back in half an hour," Chase said. "And don't let him out of your sight." The glare that Antonello got was as cold as an arctic winter.

She nodded and took Ricky's hand, leading him down the street toward the Ponte Vecchio, with Ricky smiling and waving to both of them.

"You might as well come inside," Chase said, holding the door.

Antonello went in.

"I think I deserve some answers," Antonello said, trying to keep his confusion and hurt at bay, but he failed. This was just too earthshattering for anyone.

"I don't have many for you, other than I am not going to stay here and let your family take away my son. I have his birth certificate as well as his passport, copies of the adoption papers, and Elaine's will with me. That is more than enough for me to take my son home. I will not stay here and let your family put me and Ricky through some needless hell." The stone cold in his eyes was chilling. "No one is taking my son away."

"But am I the father?" That was all he wanted to know.

"How the hell am I supposed to know? I thought Ricky's father was the jerk, Rodrigo, that she dated after you. God, I have no idea what she saw in him, other than the fact that he looked like you. So how in the hell am I supposed to know? And why would I give you or your mother the chance to find out? I won't lose my son and all I have left of Elaine because of you and that fucking *family duty* of yours."

Antonello gaped. "But if he is my son…?" he asked softly, still trying to get his mind around the central issue. "Don't I have some rights—a chance to be part of his life?"

Some of the cold in those intense blue eyes thawed a little. "Maybe. If you truly are his father. Look, I'm going to pack, and he and I are going back home. It will probably cost me my job, but I can't let you and your mother rip apart my family. I can't." The heartbreak in his voice was almost too much for Antonello to take. "I can't lose Elaine all over again." He slumped into a chair, and Antonello wondered what the hell to do. "I think you'd better go. I'm sure your mother is already getting her ammunition out and her weapons loaded for battle, and your precious family duty will require you to stand behind her."

Antonello growled and then slapped the table next to him. "Fuck it, Chase. Ricky could be my son. I had no idea he existed until I saw him and you on the Ponte Vecchio that day. If I am his father, then I deserve a chance to be part of his life. Hell, I deserve—"

"You threw all that away when you left, remember? You were gone, and we had to pick up the pieces. Shit. I should never have come here." Chase glared at him with full-on hatred. "Elaine asked me to raise her son, and let me tell you something else. She hated you until the day she died." Chase's words hit him like a punch, and he took a step back. "I don't think she hated anyone… ever… as much as she did you after you left."

"Chase… stop." He turned toward the door. "We need to figure this out. We need some answers."

Chase shook his head. "What I need to do is go back home before your mother calls out her troops and tries to stop me."

"My mother…," Antonello started as a firm knock sounded on the door behind him. They both turned toward it, and Chase crossed his arms over his chest, his entire expression screaming "I told you so."

"Go ahead and let her minions in. Then you can go, and I'll clean up the mess." Chase followed him to the door, and Antonello opened it for the polizia. His mother was never one to be patient.

"I don't know what you've been told, but I have everything documented," Chase said levelly. Antonello had to admire how calm he was when faced with two menacing uniformed officers.

"It has been reported that you are holding the grandson of Contessina Glorioso and intend to leave with him."

"I am here with my son. Whatever Contessina Glorioso thinks is irrelevant," Chase said. "I have my son's US passport and his US birth certificate, as well as copies of the adoption that took place four years ago. I also have a copy of his mother's will leaving me custody of her son after she died." He motioned the officers inside and laid copies of everything out on the table.

"Where are the originals?" the officer asked in a heavy accent. He didn't seem confident of his English.

"They are safe," Chase said, stepping back.

"And you are?" the second officer asked Antonello in Italian.

"I'm Antonello Glorioso. And my mother is overreacting. We have no proof other than a few pictures that Ricky is my son." What he needed to do was face facts and see if he could defuse this situation. Otherwise, he was convinced that Chase's documentation would hold up, and once that happened, Chase and Ricky would return to the States, and it was unlikely that he would ever see either of them again.

"I see. So your mother is unsure of this? Then why did she report a possible kidnapping? That is a very serious charge."

Antonello sighed. "You don't know my mother, and for your sakes, I hope you never do." It was the only explanation he had. His mother was willing to do what she had to for the family, and if that meant using her influence, she definitely would. "I'm sorry my mother gave you an incorrect impression, but I have no reason to contend that any of these documents are incorrect or forgeries. I'm sure they are genuine." What the hell was he going to do? Start a fight over something he wasn't sure of? It was best to calm the situation, and then maybe he and Chase could figure out a way to get the answers they needed.

The officers spoke between themselves, and then, after looking over the documents, thanked Antonello and apologized to Chase before leaving.

"What did you say to them?" Chase demanded as soon as they were gone.

"The truth. That your documents are real and that we don't know that Ricky is my son. They are not going to act on anything other than facts. And yes, my parents do have influence with the police, as well as the city government, but I only told what we really know, nothing more."

Now it was Chase's turn to collapse in a chair. "Why did you do that?"

"What?"

"I'm a foreigner, and you're the Glorioso heir. I'm sure the police would have listened to you and done what your mother wanted. Or at least they would have made trouble for me." He lifted his gaze from the floor. "So why? You could have had what your mother wanted… at least for now."

"Why would I do that? I have no proof of anything other than a few old pictures." He pulled out one of the dining chairs from the small table and sat down. "It wasn't going to change anything. If I am Ricky's father, then there are things that will have to be different. If he is my son, then he will inherit everything my family has. It is tradition, and my family is bound by that as much as it is by the law. If he is another man's child, then…." Antonello tried not to think about that possibility. "The thing is, I want to know, and not just for my family. If I am Ricky's father, then I want to be part of his life."

Chase wiped his eyes and shrugged. "So? How wonderful for you. And how does something like that work? Will your family get the happy task of saddling my son with the same kind of duty that they pressed on your shoulders? Will they obsess over him getting married to some suitable Italian girl and having babies to keep the family going? Will they expect Ricky to move here and give up the choices in life that should be his to make? Because I will not have that. Ricky is my son, and he will get to make the choices about his life that he wants. I won't have him as unhappy as you've been." He shook his head. "No. I think it's best if he and I leave the country. You can just forget all about me and Ricky. Pretend none of these things happened and go back to the life you had. I'll do the same."

"And what? Forget about the last two months, and the way you and Ricky turned my life upside down? I should just forget about the fact that you brought my heart back to life and that because of you, I actually found the courage to tell my parents who I am? Nothing can go back to the way it was. You and Ricky can leave, but I won't be able to just let go. I might have a son. Do you know how that changes everything?" He found himself on his feet and actually smiling. "Just to think there's a chance that Ricky could be my son." Hell, he felt like dancing. "That I could…." He paused because words failed him. "I've been so jealous of both of you for weeks because I knew it was unlikely that I would ever have a family of my own like that. And now you tell me that we should go back to the way things were and forget. Can you?"

Chase swallowed, and Antonello knew the doubt he saw in those eyes. "I have to protect Ricky. That's all that matters. How is he going to feel if he's torn away from the people he loves? I can't let that happen to him."

"I get that. I really do. And I've seen how happy he is. I was never that way as a child. My life was too regimented, too dictated for that. And when I got old enough, I was sent away to school." It was hard for him to imagine a life like the one Ricky had. A childhood filled with love and care rather than lessons from a tutor and a viewing with his parents in the afternoon. It was like he'd been raised in another age, and one he intended to make damned sure didn't return—not for Ricky.

"So what do we do?" Chase asked. "Your mother is not going to be happy that her initial gambit didn't work, and I'm sure she will be plotting her next move. Understand that I will not put my family in danger. That will not happen."

"And I don't want to see that." He could only imagine what his mother would try to do. She could be a real tiger when she wanted something. Both his parents carried Medici family blood, his father much more than his mother, but it was she who would have been at home with their machinations.

"But what about what your family wants? What is going to happen when they play the duty card again? No one has tested you or Ricky, but I can already tell that they are going to go to that old playbook again. It worked before." Hurt flashed in Chase's eyes.

Antonello knew that Chase was right. His mother had already set the stage, and she would use every weapon at her disposal to get him to do what she thought was best. And he was going to have to choose. "That may be true. But this is different. They are my parents, but Ricky could be my son, and whether they like it or not, he has to come first. And I want to be part of his life."

Chase nodded slowly. "I get that, but we're back to the same question. What are we going to do?"

"We?" Antonello asked.

"Yes. Unless I want to quit my job, I'm stuck here for the duration. And as much as my boss is a dick, that isn't something I'm really interested in at the moment. But I will walk away and take Ricky back to the US if your parents pull any more of what happened today. And it's your job to make that clear to both of them."

"And what about getting some answers?"

"You mean like a DNA test?" Chase asked.

Antonello nodded. "If I'm his father, then we figure out the next step, together. And if I'm not, then all of this goes away. But as long as there is doubt, my family will press for answers and try to spin things the way they want. And even if you leave the country, my parents will follow you—or at least their lawyers will."

"Is that a threat?" Chase demanded.

"No. It's just a fact." He drew closer. "Look at it this way: if Ricky is their grandson, then they are going to want to be part of his life too."

"Is that only what you want?" Chase asked.

Antonello gently cupped Chase's cheeks. "No. I want Ricky and you to be part of my life regardless of whether he's my biological son. Okay? You asked what I wanted, and that's it. So I don't quite know what the next steps are for us or how to handle this particular issue, but I know you and I will figure it out." His phone rang, and he pulled it out. "My mother."

"Go ahead and talk to her," Chase said, but Antonello declined the call. "You're going to have to face her one way or another."

"Yes." He checked the time. "But right now I need to get back to the office, and I'm afraid your boss is going to start calling or messaging. And unless you want to explain to the dickhead about Ricky and everything that's happening, we should return to the office, and after work we can sit down and figure out a plan."

"Okay." Chase got his bag just as Ricky and Bianca got back from the park. Chase hugged his son and gave Bianca strict instructions that she was to keep Ricky inside and to call if anyone came to the house. Then they walked back to the office.

Inside, Antonello went right to his office, where his father waited behind his desk. Antonello closed the doors and stepped up to the desk. "Why are you here?"

"Because your mother is driving me crazy and I needed to get out of the house. You know how she can be when she thinks she isn't getting what she believes is her due." He sat back. "I understand you were the one who kept the police from—"

"Taking a little boy away from his dad?" Antonello challenged. "I won't be part of that under any circumstances. Chase is Ricky's adopted parent, and he's Ricky's mother's brother. He has cared for him practically since Ricky was a baby, and he's the only daddy Ricky has known. How would you have felt if it turned out that you weren't my father and that someone was going to take me away from you?" he asked.

"This isn't the same thing."

"And neither is sending the police to kidnap a little boy when we don't have the facts, so Mother needs to back off. This isn't any of her business—or yours, for that matter. It's mine, and I will handle it as I see fit. I will be telling Mother that once I get home." He had had enough of his parents driving his life and his decisions. It was time he made them on his own.

His father stood and came around the desk, then pulled Antonello into a hug, something they had done maybe half a dozen times in his life. "I'm so proud of the man you've become."

Chapter 17

Chase was nervous as hell when he got back to the office. He dealt with a project team meeting, thankful that Dave ran it and once he had provided updates on his pieces he could remain quiet and half listen. As soon as it was over, he called Bianca to make sure everything was okay.

"Ricky is playing with his Legos, and we're about to have lunch," she told him.

"Thanks," Chase said, still not trusting that something wasn't waiting in the wings to add even more drama to the day. Antonello's door remained closed, and that only made Chase wonder even more. By the time his day was over, he was a nervous wreck. He left the office without speaking to Tio and quickly walked home.

Ricky ran over to see him, holding Sheepy under his arm. "Can I go outside?" he asked, practically bouncing off the walls.

"Yes. We'll go for a walk." He placed his bag on one of the kitchen chairs and thanked Bianca for her patience. "I'm sure he's been wound up."

"He's a good boy," she said, her expression not hiding her worry. "Is he going to be all right? Is there trouble?" She swallowed hard and looked at Ricky before lowering her voice. "The Gloriosos are very powerful, and they have a lot of sway here." This was her warning. "Mr. Antonello is a good man, but his mother… not so nice. If you know what I mean. She likes to get her own way."

"I understand, and thank you," Chase said, more nervous now than he had been before. "It will be all right." One way or another. Chase already had open return tickets for himself and Ricky. He had insisted on that when he took the assignment, so all he would need to do was get them on an open flight and they could be out of the country. "Thank you for everything."

She nodded. "I will see you and Ricky in the morning." Bianca left, and Chase sat down, trying to figure out what the hell he should do.

"You need to get on a plane and come home now," his mother told him when he called her after Ricky was in bed. "You are talented, and you can find a new job. This isn't worth putting Ricky in danger." Concern filled her voice. "I always knew this assignment was a bad idea." She clicked her tongue softly. "And what if Antonello is his father? Do you think these people will ever let Ricky go? They will get their hooks into him somehow and we will never see him again."

"I'm just figuring things out," he told her.

"You can do that back here where it's safe," she countered. "He left your sister, and if he is Ricky's biological father, then he abandoned both of them when he left." She sniffed, and Chase knew it was mostly fear, something he shared.

"I don't know, Mom, but I knew I needed to call and let you know what was happening here. I saw the resemblance the first time Ricky and Tio were together, but no one else seemed to until Tio's mother…."

He didn't know what to expect, but a soft laugh was not on his list. "Mothers know. She saw her child's eyes looking back at her. It was the same as soon as I saw Ricky. I saw parts of Elaine and you looking back at me." She shook her head, the Facetime camera wavering with the movement. "Whatever you do, you be careful. More than anything, I want you and Ricky home. That's all that matters."

"I know, Mom. But this is a mess that has to be sorted through. Just coming back isn't going to make it go away. I miss Elaine, but she had to know the lay of the land and who Ricky's father was."

"You can't blame her for this."

"Of course I can. She didn't tell any of us, and she had to know. She was still so angry with Tio after Ricky was born. I knew she was still hurt, but she should have told us…. I should have been able to put the pieces together." He wondered if he had just been stupid. "All of this could have been avoided."

His mother looked at him through the connection, saying nothing for a long time. "I know you were in love with him too." Chase nearly dropped the phone. "I'm your mother, remember. I know how you felt. But then he and Elaine started dating…. You were so good about it, wanting what you thought was best for her… for both of them." She sighed. "I don't have any answers, and I'm scared to death for both of you. But find out what's truly going on and get the answers you need. Don't listen to me or anyone else." She sniffed and dabbed her eyes with a tissue. "But you promise me that when this is over, you and Ricky will come home. I miss both of you."

"I know, and Ricky misses you too. This weekend, I'll put him on Facetime and the two of you can talk. I promise. And be on the lookout for an envelope. Ricky sent you some pictures that he made." They shared a smile. "I love you, Mom, and thank you for listening."

"I have your back, you know that. All you have to do is call me and I'll come over there and battle it out, mother to mother. That woman won't stand a chance."

Chase laughed. That was his mom—a real tiger. "I don't think it will devolve into a mom-on-mom cage match, but if it does, you're who I want on my team." He flashed her a quick smile.

"You better believe it," his mom said as Chase yawned. The day had been one of the most exhausting and nerve-jangling of his life. He wasn't sure he would be able to sleep, even if he did feel like he was going to fall over at any moment. "I'll let you go, but you call me if anything happens, and I will get there come hell or high water."

"Thanks, Mom," he said gently before ending the call. There had to be a way through this mess, and maybe once he wasn't completely worn out, he would be able to see it.

HE WOKE to knocking and groaned as he checked the clock by the side of the bed. It was still early. He passed by Ricky's room to check that he hadn't woken up before going to the door. He wasn't sure what to expect and half thought he'd find the police outside his door once more.

"It's awfully early," Chase told Antonello as he let him in.

"Sorry, but last night was pretty tense at home. Needless to say that my mother was not happy at all, especially when the police reported that there was nothing they could do. And you have to understand that they did not like telling her that one bit. My parents…."

"They have sway… I know. Bianca has already warned me." He looked down and realized he was in a pair of boxers and a T-shirt. "I should go get dressed."

"Not on my account," Tio said softly, his voice deep. "I like this particular view."

Chase rolled his eyes. "This isn't exactly the time for sexy talk. Your mother tried to take Ricky away, and I didn't sleep worth a damn all night. I'm worn out and beating myself up for not just getting on a damned plane and going home." He was still so wound up over it he didn't know what to do.

"I understand. I didn't sleep well either. But I did speak to my father, and he and I are on the same page. We also agreed that it's his job to keep my mother under control. Though I have no idea what that means exactly." Tio swallowed hard. "But he suggested that maybe we should have you and Ricky to dinner. We need to talk this out. My father suggested Friday evening, and I agree with him." Tio drew closer. "And that will give us a chance to come up with a plan."

"What kind of plan?" he asked as Tio wound his arms around his waist, pulling him tight against the heat of his body. "What exactly do you have in mind?"

"Lots of things," Tio growled before kissing him hard enough to roll Chase's eyes to the back of his head.

"Daddy," Ricky said from behind him, and Chase cleared his throat and backed away, feeling like a naughty teenager. "Is it time to get up?" He held Sheepy McSheeperson in one hand, rubbing his eyes with the other.

"No." He backed away from Tio. "Come on. It's still really early." He took Ricky by the hand and led him back to bed, then tucked him under the covers. "Just go back to sleep."

Ricky rolled over, hugging his stuffed sheep to him. "It's okay if you kiss Mr. Nello. I don't mind. Boys can kiss boys if they want to. Grammy says so."

"Okay. You go to sleep." He rubbed Ricky's back for a few minutes, and he settled down. Chase then left the room and quietly closed the door.

"See?" Tio was right there to pull him into a tight embrace. "Boys can kiss boys if they want to." He kissed him again. "Come on. We have a few hours before we have to be at the office, and we can make the most of it."

"We'd have to be quiet," Chase said, his willpower fading fast. Hell, Tio was right there and sexy as all hell. The truth was he didn't want to back away. What he really wanted was for these doubts and worries to go away.

"What is it?" Tio asked as Chase stood unmoving.

"I keep wondering what Elaine would think about this and if I'm doing the right thing."

Tio stroked his cheek. "Only you can answer that. Not your sister or anyone else. You're the one who is always telling me that I should follow my heart to what would make me happy. And here you are, worried about everyone else."

"Yeah…," Chase said as he tugged Tio down to his room and closed the door. "But you still have to be quiet." He chuckled as they tumbled down onto the bed, Tio slipping off Chase's shirt before sliding down his boxers, and Chase had to bite his lower lip to stay quiet as Tio did magical things to him with his lips and tongue.

"YOU LOOK tired," a deep voice said from Tio's office. Chase probably shouldn't, but he let his curiosity get the better of him.

Chase cleared his throat when he saw Paolo perched on the edge of Tio's desk. "I thought I heard you."

"I was going to see if Antonello wanted to go out, but it seems he's been keeping himself busy. Do I know her?" Paolo asked.

Tio rolled his eyes, and Chase took a step back. Tio's dealings with his friends were none of his business. It was up to Tio to decide what he wanted to tell them.

"You're the one who hasn't been around," Tio said with a smile. "Have you been busy?" Paolo nodded, and Tio smacked him on the shoulder. "Who is she?"

Paolo lowered his gaze, and Chase crossed his arms over his chest. There was a real story here. "Gemma," he finally said.

"Gianetti?" Tio asked and grinned when Paolo nodded. "My mother was trying to fix me up with her, but we never went out."

"Yeah… well. My mother invited her to dinner," he mumbled. "And we've been going out for three weeks." He seemed disconcerted.

"What's the problem?" Chase asked.

Paolo sighed like the weight of the world was on his shoulders. "I like her, and she's feisty…."

Chase grinned, and Tio actually laughed. "You got hooked, and now you're wondering if she's the right one."

"It's worse than that. Mamma swears she is, and if I actually marry her, then she will know she was right and I will never hear the end of it." He held his head in his hands. "What do I do?" He shook his head for a few seconds. "Give me some good news. Who is it that you have been seeing… and don't tell me your mamma fixed you up. My heart cannot take it."

"No, my mother most definitely did not introduce us," Tio said, looking right over at Chase. Their gazes met for a second, and Paolo followed Tio's eyes to him.

"What?" he asked. "Where's the girl?"

"There is no girl," Chase said flatly and figured he'd make it easy on Tio. "What Tio is trying to tell you is that he and I have been seeing each other."

Paolo turned back to Tio in what could only be described as an imitation of a large-mouth bass in disbelief. "No." He broke into Italian, and Tio nodded slowly. Paolo immediately went silent, and Chase held his breath, hoping like hell that Paolo wouldn't turn his back. He knew that would hurt Tio more than just about anything else. He could have taken his parents' not accepting him, but Chase saw in Tio's eyes the very beginning of heartache that grew more real and deeper the longer Paolo just sat there. "This is a joke?"

"It isn't," Tio finally said. "I've had feelings for women, but I also have them for men, and Chase most of all." He stood up, wobbling a little.

"So I guess neither of us is going to be going out to pick up women," Paolo said with a shrug. "We could go out cruising for guys, though, if that's your thing."

Chase growled, and Paolo put his hands up. "I joke."

"You better be. Gemma deserves someone to be good to her."

Paolo turned to him. "How you know what she deserve?"

Chase shook his head. "Because all women do. Sheesh. Is he another one like your cousin Lorenzo?" he asked Antonello. Tio explained in Italian, and Paolo put his hands up again.

"If he does something like that, his mamma will make sure the family line stops with him," Tio explained, and Chase nodded.

"I think I wanna meet his mamma sometime." Chase grinned, and Paolo slipped off the desk.

Paolo smiled. "She'd probably cook for you, and if you make Antonello happy, she'll love you forever." He patted the top of the desk. "My mother always adored Antonello here, and she'd want him to be happy."

"Doesn't she want you to be happy?" Chase asked. Maybe it was the language barrier, but sometimes he didn't understand these people even when they were speaking English.

"What my mother wants is grandchildren—lots of them. And she is determined to get me married so my wife can start providing them for her." He groaned and shook his head. "At least Tio has an excuse." He went to the door.

"You know, maybe the four of us could go out sometime," Paolo said, and Chase nodded. He'd like that a lot, and Tio was even smiling. "What? Did you think I'd throw you over or something?" He rolled his eyes. "Hell, bring on the gay guys. That leaves more women for the rest of us."

"I'll be sure to tell Gemma that when I see her next time," Tio said. Paolo made what Chase figured was a rude Italian gesture before leaving the office.

"I really thought he'd flip out," Tio said softly, looking after his friend. "So far things have been okay."

"Well, you haven't really dealt with your mother yet," Chase said.

"No, but she did say to come to dinner on Friday, so that is a step in the right direction. I think she wants to talk with you."

Chase groaned. "Your mother wants to roast me over a spit and pick my bones before throwing them out for the dogs in the street."

"Really vivid."

"But accurate. She would be happy if I disappeared so she could determine if Ricky was her grandson. And if he was, I bet she would figure out a way to have him raised in the same repressive way she raised you. And that isn't going to happen. I'll meet your parents and play nice, but I'm not backing down or giving up my son."

Tio closed his office door. "Of course you aren't. Now I think we need to finish up the workday. Then we can go to your place, and at your kitchen table, you and I will figure out options and a plan for dealing with all of this."

"I see." Chase hadn't ruled out getting the hell out of the country, but he was keeping that in reserve at the moment. Still, he intended to be prepared for Ricky's sake. He was the most important person in this whole situation. Chase returned to his office and closed the door, cursing Elaine quietly for leaving him in this mess in the first place.

"If you had been up front with us, then none of this would have happened and we could have avoided the entire situation." But then he would never have crossed paths with Tio again. He sat at the desk, holding his head, knowing now that having Tio in his life had so far been worth it.

Chapter 18

"YOU EXPECT me to just let our grandchild go?" Antonello's mother asked as though it was the most ridiculous thing in the world.

"Papa, help me," Antonello said, shaking his head.

"We don't know that this child is Antonello's, and even if he is, this is something that he needs to work out."

She seemed about ready to explode. "You do realize that if this is our grandson, then he gets to inherit everything from Antonello. That we can basically cut our idiot nephew out of the line of inheritance, and we don't need to worry that his wife is pregnant. This is important in securing the family legacy going forward." Her eyes blazed as she set her Aperol glass on the table.

"We realize that," his father said.

"Then do something about it."

"What?" Antonello snapped. "Rip him away from the only family he has ever known? If this is your grandson, then you need to love and care for him, not treat this boy as though he's a commodity, the way you treated me." He drained the last of his drink. "I won't have it. Chase has agreed to come to dinner tomorrow, and I expect both of you to behave and drop this Catherine de' Medici act or else I'll tell him that it isn't safe here and that he should return to the States for his and Ricky's best interests." He had kept that little threat in reserve, and it had the effect he'd been hoping for. His mother paled, and his father slowly sat down. Antonello didn't look away from his mother. "You need to realize that you are not the one in control here. I am."

"But if you let him go…."

"There are more important things than the family inheritance," he said softly. "I happen to like Chase, and Ricky is an amazing child. If he's my son, then I'm a lucky father, because he's amazing. And a lot of that is because of Chase." He swallowed hard as warmth radiated through him.

"Are you telling us that this… man…? That you expect us to accept…?" His mother was never at a loss for words. Ever.

"Yes. Chase is special to me, and he has been for a long time. I was too scared to tell you about it when I was in college, afraid of how you would react, and I was right."

"Then what changed?" his father asked gently. Antonello was coming to appreciate his quiet thoughtfulness more and more.

"I found someone—two someones, actually—who mean more than my fear." He cleared his throat. "And I came to realize that your opinion wasn't all that important. That I deserved to be honest about myself and that I wasn't going to let you and Mom dictate the rest of my life." He met his father's gaze straight on.

"Are you going to let him talk to us that way?" his mother asked, anger in her voice.

His father smiled. "Our son is a grown adult and can make up his own mind. And I for one am proud of him. I know he will look after the family interests and is more than capable of seeing the family and the business into the future."

"But—"

"That's enough, Contessina. It's time for Antonello to see things into the future and for him to make his own decisions about his life."

She held firm for a few seconds and then lowered her gaze, knowing she wasn't going to get any further. "But the boy, Ricky… he could be our grandson." He had never seen his mother close to tears before.

"I know. But that would make him Antonello's son." He stood next to Antonello's mother. "Do you remember when you were first pregnant, and my mother told us how we were going to raise our children? She even decorated the nursery and picked out names. You told her to back off and that it was our baby and we were going to make those decisions. Well, I hate to tell you this, but you have turned into my mother."

"I have not," Contessina protested, and Antonello chuckled.

"Look, we all want the same thing, but for different reasons. I don't want Chase to leave. He has only a few more months and then his project will be finished and he's supposed to go home. I don't want that to happen. I want him to stay, regardless of whether Ricky is my son."

His mother nodded. "So what do we do?"

"Well, you can start by not calling the police on him," Antonello said. "And he's coming to dinner. Be nice to him and don't scare him off. You know you can be frightening. I like him, Mamma, and so does Isabella and even Paolo. He's a good man." God, he had messed things up more ways than he could count, and now he had a chance to make it right. Antonello was not going to blow this chance.

ANTONELLO'S LEG bounced on the thick rug, and he had to intentionally stop it. Chase sat next to him on the edge of the sofa that had been in the room for three hundred years. Ricky sat on his father's lap with Chase's arms around him like Chase was afraid Ricky was going to make a break for it and run amok through the house.

Antonello's parents sat in their usual places, drinks in hand, with everyone looking at each other but no one saying a word. "That's really pretty," Ricky said, looking up to point at the ceiling fresco. "With the lady flying over everything."

Thank God the kid found something to say, or else Antonello's head was going to explode. Chase had messaged only a few hours ago to say that he didn't have someone to watch Ricky, so Antonello had said to bring him along. He had been hoping this meeting would be less stiff.

"Remember what I told you," Chase whispered.

"I know, Daddy. Don't touch anything." Ricky put his hands in his lap and leaned back. "I won't, but everything is pretty. When we go home, can you paint my ceiling like that? I want elephants and a giraffe and a polar bear. But not scary ones."

Chase chuckled. "I don't think that's something I can do, but maybe they make wallpaper that we can put up that has animals on it."

"Do you like animals?" Antonello's father asked, and Ricky began enthusiastically listing all his favorites, including lions, tigers, chickens, horses, and sheep.

"I have one of those," Ricky said.

"A sheep?" Antonello's father asked, confused.

"Yes. I sleep with him. I wanted to bring Sheepy with me, but Daddy said that wasn't a good idea. So he's at home on my bed."

"Ah, a stuffed sheep." His dad seemed more at ease.

"I have lots of stuffies. I want to get a puppy, but Daddy says that I can't get one here because we are only here on loan. But maybe when I get home and if I'm good, I can get a real puppy." He smiled and looked around. "You should have a puppy here. It's big enough, and they are good company. Unless they poop. Then it's stinky."

Antonello turned away, chuckling. The conversation was really stilted if it had gotten to talking about poop. "I never had a dog."

"Really?" Ricky asked. "Why not?" He turned to Antonello's mother. "Are you 'lergic? My friend Larry is 'lergic to dogs and cats, so his mommy got him a lizard. They keep it in a 'quarium, and it sticks its tongue out. But you can't really pet it."

Antonello's mother turned to him with a quizzical expression. "He's asking if you have allergies. And no. Mamma and Papa are not allergic to animals, they're just allergic to fun."

Ricky laughed. "No one is allergic to fun." He slid off Chase's lap and went to Antonello's father. "Are they?" He suddenly seemed confused. "You do look kind of grumpy."

"Ricky," Chase cautioned.

"No, I think we have been a little grumpy, and we should remember our manners," Papa said and then smiled. "What do you like to do for fun?"

"I play with Legos and draw pictures. And Bianca teaches me Italian." He grinned. "Ciao, mi chiamo Ricky e il mio cibo preferito è la pizza."

"That's very good," Antonello said. "I like pizza too, and so does Mamma." He winked, trying to get his mother to open up a little.

"Grazie," Ricky said and then continued on about how gelato was the best and the time they'd seen a frog by the river.

"I want Ricky to be able to speak as much Italian as possible while he's here, and Bianca has been a big help. She's his nanny during the day while I'm working, and she's studying to be a teacher."

"Why?" his mother asked.

"I want him to have the best experience possible. I know he's young, but I hope he'll remember being here and that it will be good. I never got this kind of chance when I was a kid. My family couldn't afford to travel like this, so I want to make the most of it for him."

Ricky wandered over to the small windows, looked out, and smiled. "That's the Pity Palace and the river."

Antonello went over to him and lifted him up so he could see better. "Can you name other landmarks?" he asked, and Ricky explained what everything was.

"But we can't see the dome where we climbed. That was the most funnest of all," Ricky added, and when Antonello put him down, he hurried back over to Chase.

"You climbed the dome?" Mamma asked, and Ricky bounced with excitement.

"I got to see everything. It was fun, but Daddy was scared, so I held his hand."

Chase smiled, and Antonello sat down next to him and took his hand. "It was an amazing day." He held Chase's gaze, letting his folks think what they wanted. "We've had a lot of fun since you came."

"Yes," Chase said before clearing his throat. "You know, I didn't want to come here. I didn't want to uproot our lives, and after Tio returned from college, I never wanted to see him again. I felt abandoned. Both my sister and I did. We had plans, but Tio felt that it was his duty to be here and do what you needed him to. I loved him then, but I guess it wasn't to be. At least then. But now we know who we are… both of us… and coming to Florence has been a life-changing experience."

"But what happens when you have to go home?" Antonello's father asked.

"I don't know. I don't have any answers about what the future will hold. But that is up to Tio and me." He cleared his throat. "I know I should keep my mouth shut, but I can't. I know that I'm not the kind of person you ever expected to be involved with Tio. He only told you recently about his attraction to men. I get that."

"Are all Americans so direct?" Antonello's father asked.

Chase grinned. "Probably. But I like to say what I mean. Tio and I like each other, and we're figuring things out." He turned to him, and Tio's belly fluttered at the deep attraction that shone in them.

"I see that," Mamma said flatly. "But…."

"There are no buts. Chase and I will work things out." He squeezed Chase's hand. "He is well aware of my obligations here, and I know he has some of his own." He could tell his mother wanted to ask about Ricky, but she had the grace to hold her questions in front of her probable grandson.

"Ricky, do you want to see the rest of the rooms?" Antonello's father asked, and Ricky turned to Chase, his eyes huge.

"You can go," Chase said, and Ricky bounded away. To Antonello's surprise, his father held out his hand, and Ricky took it, the two of them heading for the dining room. Tio couldn't help watching them go, and then he turned to Chase, seeing him watching as well.

"We need to know for sure," his mother said more gently than Tio would have expected. "All of us." Ricky's laughter floated in from the other room.

Chase said nothing but nodded softly, his eyes filling with fear.

"No one is going to try to take Ricky away from you, no matter what happens," Antonello said.

"But she called the police on me," Chase told him.

"I know, and it won't happen again. I can promise you that," he said, aiming the words at his mother. "You are Ricky's daddy, and I have no interest in changing that. No one is going to try to take custody away from you." He had decided that no matter what, that would be true. Taking Ricky away from Chase would be wrong, and he and his family had already done enough wrong when it came to Chase and his sister.

"But if he's your son… our grandson…."

"Then he will be raised by his daddy," Tio said, holding Chase's hand once more. For the moment, he ignored Chase's surprised expression and concentrated on his mother. "I blame this whole mess on you."

She gasped, her hand snapping to her chest. "Me?"

"Yes, you. It was you who insisted that I come back home after college. Family duty and all that. I wasn't even allowed a few years to try to build something of my own. No. I was ripped away, and if I had stayed, then I would have known if Ricky was mine, and I would have been there for him and his mother. But you and your meddling and thinking you know better than everyone else took that away from me. You took away what might have been. I know in my heart that I'm Ricky's father. I know it. I see me in him just the way you do. I didn't before, but I do now. But that doesn't matter. Ricky has his daddy, the amazing person who raised him after his mother died, the one who did what I wish I could have done. I don't blame you for all of it, but I still want you to know that it's your fault because you started the chain of events that led us here."

Her eyes were as wide as the stark white plates that had been set out for dinner. "I only did what I thought was right. Your father and I wanted you here to join and eventually run the business." Her explanation seemed halfhearted and not like her at all.

"And in the process, you may have pulled me away from my son, our legacy and the next generation of our family." He waited as she processed all of this before turning to Chase. "I know my parents want to know, and I do as well, but any test to prove or disprove Ricky's parentage is up to you. No one here is going to pressure you." Antonello's throat ached, and he stood and slowly left the room, heading to the main entrance.

"Tio," Chase said, his footfalls echoing off the stone floor. He stopped at the main door to his family home. "Did you really mean that?"

"Of course I did." He turned. "They don't hold all the blame for what happened, but they have to accept some of it, and… the answers are up to you." He pulled Chase to him. "You are Ricky's daddy. No matter what. And I am not going to change that. Get the tests, don't get the tests, none of it is going to matter."

"It will to your parents, and for what happens to your family," Chase told him in a soft voice.

"Yes. But it doesn't matter to me. What does is you and Ricky. That's what really matters." He kissed him. "Because I love you. My family isn't going to understand that now, but they will in time. You make me feel alive and special. You see me and not all the rest of the trappings that go with it."

Chase chuckled. "Of course I do. I always have." They shared another kiss until a throat cleared behind them. Antonello closed his eyes to stop himself from jumping back. Then he stepped away and faced his mother, who simply looked at both of them like she was trying to process things.

"Dinner will be ready in ten minutes."

"Okay. Thank you," Tio said and turned his attention back to Chase. "Everyone in my life seems to have this amazingly bad sense of timing."

Chase chuckled. "I can tell. We should get back before—"

"Daddy!" Ricky called as he hurried up, still holding Tio's father's hand. "There's lots more pretty stuff and more people on the ceilings." He leaned closer to Chase. "And some of them are naked." He giggled softly.

"Why don't we all go back into the lounge?" Tio's father offered, and Tio held Chase's hand, smiling to himself.

"Take Ricky in. Chase and I will be there in a moment." Antonello waited until his parents had left with Ricky before cupping Chase's cheeks in his hands. "I do love you, and I want to figure out a way to have both you and Ricky in my life. Not just for a few more months, but for always."

Chase smiled and then sighed softly. "I think I've wanted that since we were in college together. But let's see how things go." Of course Chase was cautious. He wouldn't be Chase if he were anything else. "Okay?" He smiled and brought his forehead to Tio's. "I love you too. I do." But Tio knew Chase had to decide if he could trust those feelings, and Tio was well aware that was up to him.

Chapter 19

THE REST of the dinner with Tio's parents went as well as Chase could have expected. Ricky really seemed to like Tio's father. When he showed Ricky through the house, he apparently told him stories, which Ricky shared some of before he finally settled in bed with Sheepy tucked under his arm.

"I was so scared," Chase whispered as Tio placed his hand gently on the base of his back. "What am I going to do if he is your son and not mine?" He closed the door.

"You will always be Ricky's daddy. I mean that. You raised him, and no matter what happens, I won't take him away from you."

Chase nodded. "But what happens if we do have a test and it comes back that you're his father? Your parents are not going to sit back and just accept it, no matter how they acted tonight. They are going to push because Ricky will be the future of their family—your family."

"I know how they feel, and how you feel, and it isn't going to change anything. And if Ricky isn't my biological son, then I'll feel the same about him and you." He drew Chase close. "What I want is both of you. I want us to be a family. It may not have been the one we envisioned after college, but it's still what I want."

Chase wanted to believe him more than anything. "I'm scared, but we need to know. I'll order the tests, and we can have them done. This way there won't be any doubt, and once they come back… then…." He didn't finish his thoughts, because there was no need to. He might as well face facts. There was not going to be any hiding from the truth, not now. He had heard the old adage that the truth could set you free, but in his case, it could pull away everything he had ever wanted.

"Hey, you need to stop worrying. I meant what I said," Tio told him.

Chase found himself nodding even though he didn't really believe it. "I know you do. But things have a way of changing." They had in the past, though Chase wanted to believe what Tio told him. "I won't go back on what I said. We can order the test kits and send them in. That will tell us once and for all if you are Ricky's father." And if he was, then Chase was going to have to explain that to Ricky.

"Okay." Tio agreed. "Do you want me to stay?"

Chase sighed. "I don't know. Part of me wants to be alone, but I know if I do that then I'm just going to dwell on this. I made my decision, and I won't back away from it. I just hope I'm making the right one." Tio hugged him tightly, and Chase held on to him in return. All he could do now was hope.

"Daddy, there's a box that came. Does that mean that you're going to put that swabby thing in my mouth again?" Ricky asked before clamping his mouth shut. "It tasted weird." He put his hand over his mouth.

"Nope. Those are some papers for work, and we shouldn't need to do that again." He had sent in the swab kits for Ricky, him, and Tio at the same time, and he knew he was being ridiculous, but he had checked the website every day to see if there were results. There hadn't been any news yet. "Why are you so worried about it?"

Ricky shrugged, and Chase lifted him onto his lap. "I heared you talking, and what if the tests say that you aren't my daddy no more?" Ricky leaned against him, his little body shaking.

"I will always be your daddy. Your mommy was my sister, and she wanted me to take care of you, and I always will, no matter what. I'll be your daddy, and you'll be my Ricky for always." Damn it all, he thought he had been so careful when talking about all this. He held Ricky tighter. "Okay?"

"You promise?" Ricky asked.

"I do. I promise forever." He closed his eyes and just breathed as normally and deeply as he could. "Now, how about I make some dinner and you play with your Legos for a while? After that, you can have a bath and get ready for bed." He had to keep to the schedule no matter how frazzled he was becoming.

"Okay." Ricky slid down and ran to the living room, where he dumped his Legos onto the rug. Chase got some pork out of the small refrigerator and began making dinner. He was trying to think about the cooking and not everything else when his phone dinged to indicate a new email. He expected it to be from Dewey with another question. They had been going on all week, and Chase was so tired of answering things that his boss could easily see for himself if he simply looked at the project documents.

He pulled out his phone and stared at the indicator. There were results. Chase turned off the heat and sat staring at the "test results complete" email. After a deep breath, he messaged Tio that results had been posted.

Did you look? Tio sent in response.

No. This affects you as much as me. I thought we should see them together, he responded, and Tio said that he was on his way. Chase turned the heat on for the potatoes and got them cooking once more. Ricky had asked for mashed potatoes, so that was what he was making to go with the pork cutlets.

"Mr. Nello is coming over," Chase told Ricky, who nodded and continued building some sort of tower. He wished he could be as calm, but then, there were advantages to being six years old. He finished making dinner and called Ricky to the table as Tio knocked on the door. Chase let him in and then got Tio a glass of wine before sitting down.

"Would you like a plate?"

"No. I ate at the house." Tio sipped the wine and looked around, probably for some sort of clue. Chase shrugged and set his phone on the table. "Any answers?"

"Not until Ricky goes to bed," Chase answered. "And once he's done eating, it's bath time and then a story before night-night." He smiled at Ricky and returned to his dinner, refilling his own glass and Tio's. Once they were done, he cleared the table. "I'll go run your bath, and you need to get out your jammies to put on." Ricky hurried away. "Just let me get him into bed. I don't want to talk about it in front of him. He's already heard bits and asked me if I was going to still be his daddy." Chase bit his lower lip, because damn, that had hurt.

"Did you tell him that you always would be?" Tio asked, and Chase nodded. "Then you gave him the right answer."

Chase went to run the bath, and Ricky climbed into the tub. Bathtime was usually happy, but Ricky didn't seem to feel it any more than he did, and after washing, he got out of the tub and into his dino jammies.

"Story?"

"Of course." Chase took Ricky to bed and read to him about Curious George before Ricky rolled over and fell asleep. Chase kissed him gently and left the room, feeling strange and like he was doing things for the last time.

He returned to where Tio waited and pulled out his laptop, then sat at the table with another glass of wine. He opened the message and followed the link to the results. His own were no surprise, coming back as most likely Ricky's uncle.

"What about Ricky?" Tio asked, and Chase opened it, read through the results, and then nodded at the conclusion. "Well?"

"You are his father," Chase said, nearly unable to say the words. "Elaine is his mother, and you are Ricky's biological father." He stood and wandered away, staring out the window onto the street through watery eyes.

"I have a son," Tio said from behind him. "I have a son."

"Yes, you do. But what do we tell him, and how do we tell your parents? Where in the hell do we go from here? Up until now, everything has been hypothetical, but now it's really here." He expected everything to change.

"I've given this a lot of thought," Tio told him. "I want Ricky to stay here. I want to be able to get to know him, to be part of his life." This was exactly what Chase had been afraid of. "And I want you to marry me."

Chase gasped. "What about your family? Your parents? Aren't they going to flip out?" A million thoughts raced through his mind all at once. "What am I supposed to do for a living? How?"

"Chase. All those things can be worked out. My parents will come to understand and love both you and Ricky. You'll be able to stay in the country. Ricky will be able to grow up here… with both of us. And I'll get to stay with the person I love most in the world."

Chase didn't know how to answer. This was such a surprise. "You want me to marry you because it's convenient? Because then Ricky would stay?"

"No. I want you to marry me because then we could build a life together. But if that isn't what you want…." Tio suddenly seemed rejected, and Chase didn't want that either.

"I didn't say no. I'm just a little surprised. Give me some time to think things over." That sounded too *Downton Abbey* for words, but getting married hadn't been on his radar. And as thrilled as he was that Tio had asked him, he still needed a chance to think and make the right decision.

"If that's what you want."

Chase tugged Tio into a hug. "I just need to wrap my head around it, that's all. This is a lot to deal with."

"It's not like we need to get married in the next few months. In fact, my family tends to have long engagements. My mother will insist on that so she can plan the proper celebration. Italy doesn't have same-sex marriage, but they do have a civil equivalent, so that isn't an issue." Tio had clearly thought about this.

"Can I ask… would you be proposing if Ricky's test had come back differently?"

Tio smiled, reached into his pocket, and pulled out a small box. "I had this made last week after the tests were sent in. So yes. The tests were immaterial. I don't want you and Ricky to leave. I want to be clear. You and Ricky are in my heart, and I don't want either of you to leave. So stay here with me… both of you."

Chase found himself nodding. "Okay." Tio slipped the ring onto his finger. "You know that my mother is going to go out of her mind, and I expect that once I tell her, she will be on the next plane to Florence. You are going to have to deal with my mother's version of the Spanish Inquisition."

A smile spread over Tio's face. "I'll endure anything for you. And that includes facing your mother's wrath. Hell, I say we put your mom and my mom in the same room and see what happens."

Now it was Chase's turn to smile. "With our luck, they'll make friends and we will never have a moment's privacy." Tio kissed him, and Chase melded against Tio, content and happy.

"ARE YOU crazy?" his mother asked when he called and told her. He and Tio had made love to celebrate their engagement, but Chase couldn't sleep, so he left the bed and went to the living room.

"Mom, I love him, and Tio isn't the same person he was then. You need to let go of what happened, because I have. The world has moved on, and—"

"But what he did to Elaine," she countered.

"Mom," he said softly. "Elaine did things to him too. She never told Tio that he had a son." He faced silence on the line, complete crickets. "Ricky is Antonello's son, my son… and soon to be *our* son. I know it's complicated, but I wanted to try to explain everything to you."

"Is that why you're marrying him? To make the whole custody issue easier? Because if that's it, we can mortgage the house to fight them. Just come home and we'll get ready for the legal fight of the century." Damn, she was in fine form.

"No, Mom. I love him, and I'm Ricky's daddy. If I want to go, Tio isn't going to fight me. He loves Ricky too, and he promised that he isn't going to do anything to hurt him." Chase's throat ached. "That's how I know he loves us, because he's willing to give up both of us if it will make us happy." For the first time, tears ran down his cheeks. "Can you understand that?"

"Did he really say that?" she asked, some of her fury abating.

"Yes, Mom. And we want you to come over to visit. I want you to meet his family and get to know them."

"Do they know?" she asked, calming down further.

"That we're engaged? No, not yet. He just asked me tonight." Chase couldn't help looking at the ring on his finger. "He made me a ring, Mom. It's something he designed especially for us. It's got four small sapphires in it. When I asked him why four, he said there was one for him, me, and Ricky, and a fourth for the friendship and love he had for Elaine. Losing her was like losing part of myself, but that wasn't Tio's fault. His only crime was choosing his duty to his family over Elaine, me, and a child he never knew he had."

His mother sniffled, and Chase jumped as a warm hand rested on his shoulder.

"I woke up alone and wondered where you were." Tio gently rubbed his shoulders. "Talking to your mom?" Chase nodded, his emotions so close to the surface. "Okay. Come to bed when you're done." He kissed the top of Chase's head and left him alone again.

"It's really going to be okay, Mom."

"What about your job?" she asked.

"I don't know. I'm not going to tell Dewey anything until it's closer to the time that I'm supposed to leave. I want to have options, and I want to see how things work out." He smiled to himself.

"Will you get married there?" she asked.

"I don't know where we'll have the ceremony." He figured from a legal perspective it would probably be best to marry in the States. The Italian legal system and marriage/civil unions had a few issues because of the church that could be avoided by marrying back home. "But probably back there, though I'd have to talk to Tio. Everything is up in the air."

She paused, and Chase wondered what she was thinking about. "Are you happy? Does he make you happy?"

"Yes, I am, and he does." Chase found himself smiling.

"Then I'm happy. It's going to take some time to process these changes, but if you need anything, you let me know."

He smiled. That was his mom, the tiger. "I will," Chase said before ending the call and sitting back. He sighed with contentment before returning to the bedroom. When he climbed into bed, Tio pulled him close.

"Is everything okay?"

"Yes," Chase answered as he closed his eyes.

"I heard your end of the conversation," Tio whispered. "Your mom is… concerned."

"Yes. But I think she just needs some time." Chase ran his hand over Tio's chest and down his belly. "She also asked where we'd get married."

Tio chuckled. "I think the legal part should be there. It will make things easier. I'd like to have a traditional wedding celebration here for all my friends and family so they can see that what we're doing is normal—ordinary—and the same as they do for their children."

"Okay. That was easy."

Tio sat up slowly. "Some things will be, and others will be harder. But we'll deal with them together." He rolled over and kissed Chase, pressing him against the mattress, heat rising between them in an instant. "Amore mio," Tio whispered.

"I love it when you speak Italian."

Tio said some more, but Chase didn't understand it. He was about to ask what he said, but Tio kissed him harder and then proceeded to spend a good portion of the night showing Chase exactly what he meant. And damn it all, Chase never knew Italian—or any language—could be so damned hot.

"Tell me more," Chase asked, he had no idea how much later, covered in sweat as Tio stretched over him, moving slowly, filling him. Tio whispered in Italian, his tone deep, the words falling over Chase. It didn't matter what he said—all that counted was the deep, rich voice, the heat between them, and the feel of Tio as he moved deep inside, touching his heart just as surely as his fingers stroked his chest before wrapping around his length, stroking him and sending Chase on a journey of passion that he hoped to God would never end. This was a beginning for them, and it was one hell of an amazing way to start.

Chapter 20

"WILL YOU be home tonight?" Mamma asked as Antonello got ready for work. He had stopped at the family home to get a few things.

"I doubt it," he told her.

"You've spent much of the last month away," she said.

"Because I'm happy there." He grabbed a bag from his closet and began filling it with the things he'd need for a few days.

"And you aren't here?" she pressed.

"Mamma. You have to understand that I am forging my own life, and that will be what I say it is. I have asked Chase to marry me. He will be my husband, and you need to accept it. Papa has. I am not going to live the life that you want or according to your wishes. I won't. I'm staying with Chase and Ricky because they are the life I want." He set the bag aside. "I know you are having a difficult time with this, but it's like swimming upstream when the Arno is flooding. You get nowhere." He took her hands. "I want your support. I really do. You're my mother. But I won't beg for it, and I won't change my mind. We want you to be part of our family."

She shook her head. "You don't. You want everything as you will."

"Yes. And this is my life, mine and Chase's, and that's how it will be. There are things in this world that none of us get to decide. But this is something I got to choose, and I won't back down." He lightly squeezed her hand. "This is not your decision to make. The only thing you get to decide is whether you will be part of our lives… and your grandson's life." Ricky and Antonello's father were already fast buddies. His father had joined them for some of their outings in the city, while his mother had demurred. And every Sunday, Ricky and his Nonno went for gelato together, just the two of them. "That's what we all want… and I know you do too, even if you're too stubborn to admit it." He kissed her cheek and went back to packing.

"Okay. I will try," she said.

"That's all I ask." He smiled at her.

"I wonder what people are going to say."

That was an admission Antonello thought he would never hear his mother make, and he relaxed a little at her honesty. "They will take their cue from you. So if you're supportive, they will be as well. After all, you are Contessina Glorioso." He grinned, and his mother finally broke a smile. "Chase's mother is coming next week, and I want her to meet the two of you."

His mother nodded. "I think I'd like that."

"Good."

"And maybe I can join your father this Sunday when he takes Ricky for gelato."

Antonello let out a silent sigh of relief. "I'm sure Ricky would love to get to know his nonna." He closed his bag, and after giving his mother a hug that seemed to surprise her, he left the room and headed out to the office.

USUALLY ANTONELLO and Chase had lunch together, but Chase had things he needed to do, so Antonello brought him something back and placed it on his desk. "What is it?" he asked at Chase's stunned expression.

"Just a minute," Chase said, setting down his phone. "Dave, I'm here with the head of Glorioso. Do you want to explain what's going on to him?"

"Of course," Dave began. Antonello knew Dave as the head of the project, a coworker of Chase's, but they had never actually met. "Dewey, our supervisor, was let go yesterday. He wasn't performing the way that was expected, and he was walked out of the office toward the end of the day. I have been asked to replace him."

Chase nodded. "You deserve it."

"Thanks, Chase. I knew this was coming because I was already felt out, but I could say nothing."

Chase nodded and seemed to understand. "Of course. Does this change what we're doing here?"

"No. We still need you there in Florence. This project must continue and stay on track. It's been the only bright spot in the mess I've inherited."

"I see." Chase motioned Tio over and took his hand.

"Once you come back, I want to see about you taking over this entire project. I need someone I can count on to see it through to the end."

Chase cleared his throat. "I'm willing to do that as long as I can manage the project from here." Tio squeezed Chase's fingers. "See, Dave, I'm getting married."

"And let me guess. The person you've met is there."

"Dave, the person I met is the head of Glorioso. Antonello and I knew each other in college, and we have rekindled our feelings for each other. I'd like to keep my job with Smithson, but I'd need to do it from over here."

"Congratulations," Dave said with sincerity.

"I understand if that isn't going to work. You probably need to talk things over with the higher-ups and discuss what you want to do. But I will be staying here."

"What if that isn't going to work?"

"Then Chase will come to work for us," Tio cut in. "We are looking to expand our presence in the US, and we will use his skills to build up our business there." He grinned. "So either way, he will come out on top, but I think it would be a shame for you to lose someone of Chase's talents." He left the office, closing the door between them to let Chase finish up his call.

He got to work and waited for Chase to come in once he was finished. "Are you serious? You make me a job offer without talking to me about it first?"

"I did no such thing. I just ensured that Smithson will want you and will probably be looking to give you a raise. They're like boys with toys. They only want something when someone else wants it too. Besides, if they are dumb enough to let you go, then we will figure something out."

Chapter 21

RICKY SAT on the sofa, looking up at Chase with huge eyes filled with confusion. "Is Mr. Nello my daddy?" He chewed his lower lip. Chase had done his best to try to explain what was going to happen.

"No. I'm still your daddy, and like I told you before, I always will be. You know that I'm also your uncle because your mommy is my sister. And back in college, Mr. Nello and your mother loved each other. So he is your father." His head ached.

"And now Mr. Nello loves you and you love him?" Ricky asked, and Chase nodded. "So you're going to get married."

"Yes. And your grandmother is going to be there, and she is going to be coming over here to see you." He smiled, hoping that this wasn't too much for him. "She'll be here tomorrow." He had spent the past week trying to figure out what to say to Ricky and just basking in the warm glow of Tio's love and care. It had been a whirlwind both at work and here. Tio's parents had invited them again for dinner, and Contessina had been less reserved. She wasn't exactly warm, but maybe some of the frost was starting to melt, at least as far as Ricky was concerned. Tio's father really seemed to be taken with grandfatherhood, and Ricky adored him in return.

Ricky sat for a few seconds. "Yay. Can I make a picture for her?"

Chase shrugged. He had expected more questions. "Sure. Go make pictures for everyone."

Ricky slid off the sofa and hurried away, and Chase sighed happily. "We need to go in half an hour," he cautioned Ricky. "We're having dinner at Isabella's. And you can play for a while."

"Okay."

Chase felt damned lucky.

A knock sounded, and Chase let Tio inside. "What's going on? You look stressed."

"No. I'm fine. I think I explained things to Ricky, and he's off drawing pictures. How are you?" he asked, and Tio kissed him.

"Better now," he said softly. "Paolo called, and he's going to join us for dinner. He's bringing Gemma." Tio was pleased. "I think this is really serious. He's dated girls before, but they always passed through. Gemma seems to be sticking."

"That's great," Chase said.

"Then why so tense?" Tio asked.

"Did you forget that my mother is arriving tomorrow? I have done my best to explain things, but…."

"She still sees me as I was in college," Tio said. "Don't worry. Everything will be fine. We are not the same. We have lived life since then. Your mamma will see that, and what she wants most is for you to be happy."

"And you make me happy." That was for damned sure.

"You also know that once the mothers get to know each other, they are going to start planning the wedding," Tio added, and Chase growled. That was the last thing he wanted to think about at the moment. The amount of work… the decisions. "Just let them. My mother has been waiting for years to do this. Besides, I have it all worked out."

"You do?" Chase asked.

"Yes. Italy does not have marriage for people like us. It is similar, but not the same. So we get married in the US, so it is legal there. Then we register here in Italy to make sure we are safe. Then we celebrate." He grinned, and his eyes filled with happiness that carried Chase right along with it.

"Perfect." He bit his lower lip.

"Then what is bothering you? Is it me?"

Chase had been trying to hide it.

"No. I'm just on edge because Smithson hasn't yet told me what their plans are and if they'll let me stay here. I like my job." He turned to Tio. "While I appreciate that you and your father would make room for me in the company, I'd really like to have my own job and make my own way. Do you understand?"

Tio held him tighter. "My father is going to respect you more for that, and I only want you to be happy. Though know that the offer is still open if you need it. Either way, we hope that you will help us. Because of the deal with Smithson, we are getting more business in the United States, and we are looking to increase it even more."

"Of course I'd help. We're all going to be a family."

Tio ran his fingers through his hair, cradling Chase's head. "Yes, we are. And I was thinking that while your mother is here, we should all go down to the villa in Rome for a few days."

Damn, his life was going to be so much different from what he was used to. "You're going to spoil us, you know that?"

"Yay," Ricky called from behind him, and Chase jumped slightly. "I'm going to get my bathing suit."

"Ricky, we aren't leaving right now," Chase said and began to laugh. Their lives were going to be different, but as much as that might have worried Chase once, now it only filled him with warmth. "I'd better go see what he's up to. He might be packing already."

Tio chuckled warmly, and Chase reluctantly slipped out of his embrace to see what his son was up to.

DINNER WAS amazing, as usual. Isabella really outdid herself. Maybe she was trying to butter up Paolo and Gemma, but from what Chase could see, they didn't need it. Paolo and Gemma really seemed to have hit it off. The way Paolo couldn't seem to pull his gaze away told them he was definitely more than a little smitten.

"Ricky, it's almost time for us to go home," Chase said.

"Do we have to?" Ricky asked.

Chase nodded. "Ten more minutes." Ricky sighed like the weight of the world had just descended on his shoulders. Still, he didn't argue, just went back to playing whatever ball game he and Isabella's boys had made up.

"We are glad you are staying," Isabella said as she cleared away the dessert dishes. Chase helped her and got a good case of side-eye for doing it, but she didn't scold him.

"I'm glad to be staying too." He turned to Tio and shared a smile before following Isabella inside. "I'm happy here."

"This is a nice place to live, and you and Tio will be good together. I can tell. He is… how you say… I don't have the words in English."

"He's settled in his skin. He knows who he is and can be content with it."

"Exactly. And you make him that way." She set down the dishes and took Chase's hands, giving him an unexpected hard stare. "But if you hurt him I will fillet you like one of my fishes."

"Understood." Chase chuckled and could have sworn that she gave him the evil eye. "I love Tio and have since we were in college, though I never had the guts to tell him until now."

"He was not ready then," Isabella said. "Tio was not settled in his skin, like you say. He had to take the wrong path before he was ready for the right one. And in the end, Tio's path brought both of you to Ricky, and then back to each other."

She shooed him out of her kitchen, and Chase returned to the table and sat next to Tio, who carded their fingers together.

Paolo and Gemma were lost in each other's eyes, sipping prosecco. Chase lifted his own glass, holding it up, and Tio did the same. "To love," Chase whispered. "And to the twisty road that brought us back together."

Tio tapped his glass, the soft tink sound filling the small square surrounded by buildings that had been there since the Renaissance. "To love. *My* love," Tio added, and then kissed him as the shadows that had witnessed centuries of lovers purpled over them.

Epilogue

CHASE WAS all smiles as he stood next to Tio while everyone milled around the lawn of the Boboli Gardens. They made their way inside and sat at their places at the head table, with Paolo next to Tio, and Dave, who had come over with his family for the wedding, on the other side of Chase. Ricky sat at the table right in front between his Grammy and Nonno as he'd specifically requested.

"I expected there to be a number of people who sent their regrets," Tio said as they looked out at the very full gathering. "Very few people did."

"I'm glad." Chase figured that made things much easier for Contessina, who had been warming over the past year. Chase had figured out that she was very much concerned with what others, especially those in her social circle, thought of her. The celebration of their life partnership had made things much easier for her to accept. Well, that and the fact that their relationship included her only grandson, who she was coming to adore.

A light tinking sound silenced the crowd, and Tio's father stood near their table, welcoming everyone and thanking them for coming. Then he sat, and the food was served. And what a meal it was. The courses came and went, with the meal taking almost two hours, followed by Paolo's speech and then one by Tio's father. Then music filled the night with magic.

"I think they're waiting for us," Tio whispered, and Chase let him lead him to the floor before they began their first dance. It was magical, and after a few minutes, Tio motioned to his parents to join them. Soon the floor was filled with couples, including Ricky dancing with Chase's mother.

"Are you happy?" Tio asked softly.

"More than I ever thought possible." He closed his arms around Tio's neck and rested against him, letting the music carry him away. They had decided on a delayed honeymoon, given their recent trip to the States. Both of them had plenty to do, with Chase beginning a new project for Smithson. They had found that having someone in Europe was immensely beneficial. Instead of running his own initiatives, he spent most of his time facilitating other projects, looking to source components from Glorioso. He loved his job and the flexibility he had to work from anywhere, which meant they spent as much time at the villa outside Rome as they did in Florence.

Ricky came over, and Chase lifted him into his arms, the three of them dancing together. "Smile, Daddy. You too, Papa." They turned to where the photographer stood, and all three of them smiled. Their first official family picture. "You gotta kiss," Ricky giggled, and Chase and Tio each kissed one of Ricky's cheeks. The photographer captured Ricky mid giggle. "Not me," Ricky clarified, and Chase leaned in and kissed Tio gently as Ricky grinned. Chase knew that not everything would be easy, but for now, it was perfect.

Keep reading for an excerpt from
Noble Intentions
by Andrew Grey.

Chapter 1

"Robert," his aide, Blake, said as he knocked on the frame beside the open door to Robert's tiny office.

"Am I late for another meeting?" Robert looked up from his computer, where he'd been preparing the documents on a case for a client whose landlord was trying to evict her improperly. The guy was a real piece of work, and Robert was determined to win her some relief from the local council.

Blake chuckled softly. "No."

Robert breathed a sigh of relief and continued typing as fast as he could. He was scheduled to meet with the council in less than an hour, and he wanted to make sure he had all his arguments in place.

"But there is someone here to see you. A solicitor from London." Blake sounded half-breathless with excitement—probably wondering what was going on and if he could increase his stature in the office rumor mill.

Robert closed his eyes and tried to think if he had had any business or clients that would precipitate a visit from a colleague in London. Robert was technically a barrister, trained to argue cases in front of the courts. But here on the edge of Cornwall, Robert had decided that rather than go into high-powered practice in London, he'd become an advocate for those without the means to advocate for themselves. So he'd gone into practice with a few like-minded friends from school, and they'd opened their office on the second floor of a run-down building in Smithford. In their practice, they took everything and did everything. Two of his partners were solicitors, and Robert had learned the ins and outs of that profession as well.

"Give me five minutes, please."

Blake nodded, and Robert put the last touches on the argument and then saved the file. He'd just finished when Blake led in a man about Robert's age, spit-and-polished, wearing a suit that cost as much as Robert made in a month. Robert stood to meet the man.

"Robert Morton? William Montgomery. I'm here on behalf of your uncle, the Earl of Hantford."

"My uncle…." Robert didn't honestly remember having an uncle, but then again, his mother's family had not been the most accommodating when she'd married Robert's father. No one had talked about his mother's family in so long that they didn't register immediately in his memory. "Yes…?"

"Yes. Your uncle, Lord Harrison Hantford, the Earl of Hantford…." He paused. "Apparently the family changed their last name to that of the estate some six generations ago. He recently passed away, and under his will, you are his heir. The estate is entailed, which means your uncle didn't have a great deal of choice in the matter. You are his closest living male heir, and as such you are entitled to the earldom, as well as all the property associated with it."

Robert shivered slightly and blinked in near disbelief. He motioned for Mr. Montgomery to sit down, remembering his manners through the complete shock. "So you're saying I'm the Earl of Hantford now?" He sank into his chair and wondered what kind of holy hell had befallen him.

"Yes, sir. Or I should say, your lordship." Mr. Montgomery seemed to be taking little delight in this.

"Did you know my uncle?" Robert asked.

"I'm afraid I didn't. He was a client with Rhodes, Wentworth, and Middleton for many years, and the task of notifying you fell to me."

"I see." Robert's analytical mind began to kick in. "So what exactly has my uncle left me?"

"There is the family estate, Ashton Park, and a home in London. I'm at a loss to tell you much about them. I haven't seen either property myself, but I will be happy to meet you in the coming weeks to take you to visit them, as well as discuss any arrangements you'd like to make for the properties and contents," Mr. Montgomery said, very businesslike, which was both a relief and unsettling for Robert.

"Can you tell me if the estate is healthy?"

Mr. Montgomery chose that moment to break eye contact, and immediately Robert knew the answer. "I don't know the particulars, but I am under the impression that your uncle lived in the home in London and that he rarely visited Ashton Park. As to more details on the state of the place, we'll have to assess that when we go see it." It was a diplomatic answer, which probably meant that he'd just inherited a huge money-sucking country house with very little means to support it.

"All right." Robert had no idea in hell what else to say. He was a man who made his living with words, and he was at a near complete loss. "Thank you so very much."

"Would you like to meet tomorrow? I can at least take you to Ashton Park so you can see it. I will also have a number of papers and documents that I will need you to sign."

"Is there anyone else who has a potential claim on the estate?" Robert asked.

"No. Your uncle married, but the earl and his wife had no children. I understand from the more senior colleagues in my firm that that was a great sorrow to both of them. However, other than a few impressions and details, I don't have much information to give you. The earl's business was handled by one of our partners who recently passed away unexpectedly, and I'm stepping in to try to fill his rather large shoes." Mr. Montgomery sounded excited about this opportunity, but Robert also saw a touch of fear in his eyes, which would help keep him on his toes. Robert understood that kind of fear; he experienced it on a regular basis. Failure could be lurking everywhere, so it was to be guarded against and held at bay by always being at one's very best.

"All right." Robert pulled up his calendar and figured he could clear part of his schedule for the following day. He arranged a time, and Mr. Montgomery left his office.

Somehow Robert managed to get his mind back on his work, but not without a great deal of effort.

THAT EVENING, after a successful local council meeting that granted him everything he had wanted for his client, Robert pulled up to his mother's small cottage on the outskirts of town. She and his father had saved for years to buy their dream home. His mother, who was approaching seventy, still tended the garden and lovingly cared for the house the way she always had and showed no signs of slowing down.

"How was your day?" She gave him a fright when she popped up from behind one of the garden gateposts, where she had apparently been wrestling with some stubborn weeds.

"God." He stepped back and took a breath to still his heart. "It's getting a little late to be working out here, Mum."

"Pish," she said dismissively. "When you're as old as I am, you take your bursts of energy when you can get them." She dropped the weeds she was holding on the pile she'd collected. "Let's have a cup of tea."

"Good idea." He followed her inside and sat on one of the kitchen chairs, watching his mother put a kettle on. He remembered the dining room furniture from when he was a child. His father had made the table and chairs for his mother as a wedding present, and they had been a part of the family for as long as he could remember.

"What brings you by?" She plugged in the electric kettle and got down the cups and pot so they would be ready.

"It seems that your brother passed away."

She patted the table a few times. "Harrison is dead." She said the words in the same tone that she did when she talked about her neighbor, who she referred to as "the damned old randy bastard" on a regular basis. She smiled for a second and then turned to him. "Christ on the cross."

"You got it in one, Mum."

"But I was disinherited, and…." She sank into the chair across from him. "So my arse of a brother ended up with what he wanted anyway."

"Excuse me?" Robert said, trying to follow all of this.

"My brother was many things—pompous, arrogant, a pain in the arse know-it-all who thought since he had the title, he also had the right to make decisions for everyone else." The kettle was done, and she got up and poured. Robert waited until she was ready to continue. She brought the tea tray with pot and cups to the table and set it down gently. She filled the cups, knowing already how he took it, and handed him his. "My parents died when I was nineteen. So Harrison inherited the title and became head of the family. He thought two things. First, that the title gave him the right to dictate everything about my life. And second, that we'd stepped back a hundred years and that he ruled the damn roost, as well as my personal life. The idiot." She took a sip, pinkie out, as genteel as possible.

"Why didn't I ever hear any of this before?"

She set down her cup. "I dated a friend of my brother's for five years. He was also titled, with a lot of money. Harrison was so excited. He thought we'd marry, but the reason we dated for so long was because I wasn't ready. Then I met your father. George, the guy my brother wanted me to marry, was as pompous as Harrison. He'd hired your father to do some restoration work at his home, and I took one look at him and that was it. Your father stole my heart with a wink, a smile, and one peek at his gorgeous backside." She giggled, and Robert was glad he didn't have a mouthful of tea at that moment.

"So you dumped George and married Dad."

"Yes. In a way. I announced that I wasn't going to marry George and that I loved Peter with all my heart, and Harrison went into a rage.

He was always a control freak. Now I think he was deranged and needed professional help. But he hadn't gotten any then. When I didn't back down, he disowned me, and I turned my back on the arsehole forever."

"Mum, I think you're losing me a little."

"I'm getting to the good part. See, Harrison married soon after that, and they supposedly settled down into wedded bliss. But it seemed Harrison had bigger problems. His plumbing wasn't completely functional, and he could never have children." She snickered. "Served the old jackass right, and it's a blessing for the human race. At least his bastardness won't be passed on to anyone else." There was no mistaking her sense of glee at the turn of events.

"Mum!" He had never heard such vehemence from his mother.

"He had the audacity to approach me about returning to the family after your father died—if I let him groom you to take over for him. I told him to stuff it. You had your own life and didn't need the mess that he wanted to heap on you." She sighed. "But he did it anyway. If he weren't dead, I'd wring his neck."

"When was that?"

"About five years ago. He was in one of those regretful phases, but I knew it was a load of garden fertilizer. He never did anything without getting something for himself. And your father had just died, and I thought he was trying to take you from me and…." Her lower lip quivered, and Robert stood to gently place his hands on her shoulders. His mother was many things, but touchy-feely wasn't one of them. She placed a hand on his, and Robert gave her a chance to compose herself.

"Why didn't you tell me any of this before?"

"Because I didn't want you to have anything to do with him. Harrison was an awful man, and we had a good life here. Your father was an amazing provider. He worked hard and made his furniture to help ensure we had some of the extras." She squeezed his hand once, then dropped hers and looked up at him. "I wasn't—"

"It's okay, Mum." Robert waited for her to take a breath. "I wish you had told me, but you're right. We had a good life, and if your brother was as big a jackass as you describe, then we were better off without him."

"But now you're the Earl of Hantford."

"It seems so."

"And everything that goes with it." She turned back to her tea. "I tried to keep you from all that. I really did."

He wasn't sure what his mother was referring to, but it only added to his sense of nervousness. "I'm meeting the solicitor tomorrow, and we're going to the estate. Do you want to come with me?" *It would be really nice not to go alone.* "I'll understand if you'd rather not."

"Where are you meeting him?"

"At my office at one."

"Then I'll go with you. We can meet for lunch, and I'll tell you what I know about what you'll be walking into. Granted, my information is a little out-of-date." She motioned for him to sit, and Robert complied and finished his tea. "This is a burden I had hoped to try to spare you."

"Mum, I'm an earl and I have a peerage…. It's—"

"A burden unlike anything I think you understand." She sighed. "All I wanted for you was a life filled with happiness and the ability to make your own decisions and live your life the way you wanted. Harrison never understood that. He always thought his way of thinking was the only way and that everyone wanted the same things he did. Now he's pulled you into the mess I'm sure he created."

"We don't know the state of things."

"No, we don't. But we're going to find out." She poured another cup of tea, stood, and opened a nearby cupboard. She pulled out a bottle of whiskey and dumped a healthy dollop into her tea.

Things must have been bad. There had been only one other time that he'd seen his mother do that, and it had been the morning of his father's funeral. She had said that she needed some false courage to get through that day, and it seemed she required another dose.

"I'll see you for lunch, though I suspect I'm not going to have much of an appetite."

"I doubt things are as bad as all that." Robert stood and kissed her on the cheek before leaving the cottage. He stopped in the garden on the way out, admiring some of her flowers in the late evening light, and then walked to his car.

ROBERT FELT as though he had been through a meat grinder. He hadn't slept all night and had gone into the office early so he could get as much done as possible. He'd worked with Blake to rearrange his schedule so he could have the afternoon out of the office. Of course, with his mother in the car, he wasn't able to make calls the way he normally would.

The estate was nearly an hour west from Smithford, and he followed William's black hearselike car. His mother had been surprisingly quiet for much of the trip until they turned a corner and the top of a turret broke the skyline.

"That's it."

"When was the last time you were here?"

"Just before I married your father, so over forty years ago." She gasped when Robert made the turn and the estate came into view.

William pulled to the side of the road, and Robert followed. He parked, got out of the car, and walked up to William. His mother decided she wanted to stay where she was.

"That's Ashton Park." William waved his hands in all directions.

"How much land is there with the place?" Robert asked.

"A lot. It's the one true asset of the earldom. There is plenty of land, and from what I can gather from my colleague's notes, your uncle refused to sell any of it, no matter how difficult things got."

"How badly is the place mortgaged?" Robert asked, afraid as hell of the answer. He expected it to be up to the rafters.

"That's the thing. We can't find any record of one anywhere."

"What? You mean I own this pile free and clear?" How in the hell could that be possible? There had to be a catch, and in the back of his mind, Robert latched on to exactly what it could be. "The taxes. Forget I asked."

"Yes, sir. They are going to be steep on the manor house and all the land. However, since your uncle managed to pay the inheritance duties from when he received the estate, you only have the ones to pay for this transfer of ownership."

Like that was a comfort. Instantly upon his uncle's death, Robert owed millions in death taxes on a place he hadn't known existed, other than in some picture he might have seen on one of those documentaries they did on country houses and such.

"Well, we may as well see just how bad a state the old place is in." He tried to think of what he was going to do with it. Selling was the first thing that came to mind—if that were even possible.

"Yes, my lord," William said, and Robert stopped him.

"I'm Robert. Please call me that. I'm not going to stand on all the ceremony and crap, okay? I was Robert before you told me this news and I'm still Robert now."

"Okay." William smiled for the first time. "I'll do whatever I can, Robert."

Robert turned back to the estate and groaned. "Let's go see what we're dealing with." He got back in the car and followed William through the old gate and up the weed-scattered drive, toward the front door. "This place is…." Robert didn't quite know what to say.

"I grew up here," his mother said. "This was my home for much of my younger years."

Robert stopped, and they both got out, the gravel crunching under their feet. The façade of the building looked to be in fine shape. The stone was discolored but appeared intact.

"Is there anyone here?" Robert asked.

"Yes. There is a caretaker on the property. He lives in one of the other homes on the property and sees to it that the building itself remains in reasonable care. But little else seems to have been done in some time." William produced a huge set of keys that looked like something to open a medieval jail. He unlocked the front door and held it open for Robert and his mother.

Robert stepped inside and gasped. All the shutters had been drawn, and everything was covered in sheets and drapes that looked like dusty old ghosts as the breeze from outside fluttered into the hall. Paintings, chandeliers—everything was draped and covered. But even under the dust and sheets, the grandeur of the entry hall shone through.

"My God."

"This used to be…." His mother came inside. "I remember greeting guests as they arrived. Your grandparents were very social people and loved to entertain. It's what this house was built for. Harrison used to love his parties as well, but his took on a very different tone." She walked to the left and pushed open the door to a paneled living room with heavy molding, where a rug lay rolled up to one side. More sheet ghosts and drapes covered everything, and the floor was so dusty, it was hard to see the wood.

Robert looked up and gasped at the frescoed ceiling. "At least that's in one piece. How could anyone just leave all this to rot?" He moved into the living room and through to the next, which was a bookless library.

"What happened to everything? These shelves were full." His mother sounded as though she were going to cry as she wiped her fingers through decades of dust on an empty shelf.

"Apparently they were moved to some sort of storage," William said. "There was a bill for it in the estate records."

Robert lifted his gaze once again and knew the reason for moving stuff to storage. The expansive coffered ceiling was pockmarked with yellow stains. He closed his eyes and groaned. "The roof is going. Some of those stains are recent."

"I did me best, my lord."

Robert turned to find a man in his fifties standing in the doorway, hat bunched in his hands. "Robert Morton." He held out his hand, and the man who Robert assumed was the caretaker stepped forward nervously.

"Gene Parget, my lord. I noticed the room was leaking, so I went up and patched it best I could. I think I stopped the water coming in for now. But some damage was done, mainly in the bedroom above this one. But I don't think I can patch it much more. It needs replacing."

"What about the electrics?" Robert asked.

"That and the plumbing are going too, sir. I don't like to turn on the lights because…." He shrugged. "And the water is off to the entire manor in case of leaks."

"So what you're telling me is that this huge pile of a place needs electrics, plumbing, a roof, as well as…." He raised his eyebrows. "Is there anything that's in good shape?"

"The walls, sir. They're thick and strong, and I repaired the windows last year. Took out the bad ones, reglazed them, and then put them back. I do that every other year."

"What about the kitchen and bathrooms?" When Gene just looked down at the floor, Robert had his answer, and God knew what in the hell he was going to do. "Please show us the rest of the house, and don't leave anything out," he told Gene.

His mother moved back into the living room as Gene led Robert out of the library.

Gene showed him room after room of haunting neglect. Wallpaper peeled from many of the upstairs bedrooms, and the nursery sat frozen in time, like it was waiting for children that had gone and were never coming back. "The summer is humid and the winter cold. I did me best to care for the place, but I'm just me and—"

"It's all right, Gene. You have done the best you could, I'm sure. No one is blaming you for this." He sighed as he looked at the dust and grime covering dinge and neglect.

"Yes, my lord."

"Don't call me that, please." He was never going to get used to that. "I'm Robert. I may have inherited a title, but I believe that men should earn respect, not be given it because they happen to have been born into the right family." Robert turned and wandered through the last rooms, seeing more of the same. The room above the library was the worst so far. The plaster was cracked severely, and parts of the ceiling were in need of stabilization. He didn't go inside and closed the door after a quick peek. "Let's go back down. I think I've seen enough. What other buildings are there on the grounds?"

"There are the stables, which are empty. There's the motorshed, which is also empty. There were greenhouses, but they have fallen down. There are cottages in the village that are part of the estate. They have tenants, and part of their rent agreement requires that they maintain them. I've ensured that has happened. Then there is the park, the thousands of acres around the manor."

Robert nodded, trying to make sense of all this. Mostly what he'd inherited was a money pit. Yes, it wasn't mortgaged, and maybe he could do that, but then he needed the place to generate revenue, which wasn't going to happen with it in this condition.

"Thank you," he said absently. He'd seen more than enough of the mess his uncle had heaped on him.

He met his mother in the hallway, where she peered under sheets and dustcovers. He caught her eye and nodded, and they made their way to the door.

"I know this is a lot to take in and it's going to take some time to get the estate settled," William said as they walked out the front door.

"I know. Not that it's going to make a great deal of difference." Robert needed to figure out what in the hell he was going to do with a place that was so out of step with any sort of modern lifestyle that it threatened to raise a headache the size of London. "Gene, thank you for everything you've done and continue to do. I appreciate it." He shook the caretaker's hand once again and then led his mother to his car. He got in and lowered his window as William approached.

"I'd like to review the rest of the estate details with you soon. There is the house in London, as well as a few other assets."

"Please tell me there is some money somewhere to do something with all this." As overwhelming as all this was, he wasn't above begging if necessary.

"There is enough in various trusts to continue what your uncle was doing. The principal in the trusts can't be touched and it provides an income.

I believe that pays for the caretaker and the storage of the books and things. But other than that, no. What money your uncle had, he left to someone else." At that moment, William was as stoic as any good lawyer had to be.

"Okay. I'll need to catch up. Can we meet on Monday?"

William nodded, stepped back from the car, and went to lock the front door of the house.

Robert slowly pulled away. As he drove through the gate, the weight on his chest lifted slightly, but not very much. "What do I do with it?" Robert asked.

"The rooms are still furnished. Almost all of it is still there," she said with a sense of awe.

"All of what?"

"That manor has been in our family for ten generations. You are the eleventh, and the things they collected over the years were all added to the manor. I was afraid Harrison would have sold them, but that probably took more energy than he was willing to spend. So it's all there."

"Okay." Robert turned onto the road back to his office. "So I could sell the furnishings, and break up the land and sell that as well. That would pay the taxes and leave an empty building that could be sold or added to the National Trust if I could get them to take it." He glanced at his mother, who looked about to cry.

"That's your history, my history, and you'd do that without a second thought?" She wiped her eyes, and Robert tried to remember the last time he'd seen his mother cry. He had a hard time doing it. She never cried—stiff upper lip and all that. "You can't just throw it away offhand."

"Then what do I do? I can mortgage the place to the hilt and try to do the repairs that need to be made, but how in the hell do I pay the money back? The estate doesn't have much income, and I can't just open it to tourists and have them flock to the place like it was Downton Abbey. A few people might come, but not enough to make it worthwhile. I could just donate the whole thing to the National Trust and make it their headache, but then everything would be gone." And that was going to break his mother's heart. He could see that.

Robert pulled to a stop at an intersection and waited for a truck loaded with hay to pass before making the turn and continuing on.

"There has to be a way to do something." She was thinking already, he could tell.

"I'm going to have to see what else I've inherited and then try to figure out what can be done." Thankfully the estate wasn't too far away from where he and his mother lived. He could at least continue to live without having to make commutes halfway across the country. "I'm not going to make any decisions today or tomorrow." Robert grew quiet as he drove the rest of the way back to his office.

"I've been thinking," his mother said with a weird smile that Robert was having trouble reading. "You need money to fix up the estate, and you also have a title."

"Okay. I have a title that doesn't help me, other than make me sound like a toff."

His mother leaned closer. "That title comes with a peerage and it has power. People respect the titles. Good or bad, they do, and the title has value."

"Okay. So do I sell it?" Robert asked, knowing he was being ridiculous.

"Of course not. Well, maybe in a way. You do what the aristocracy has always done when they needed money. You marry it."

Robert turned off the engine and blinked in disbelief. "You know I'm gay, Mum. I'm not going to marry a woman."

"No. But I bet there is a gay man with a lot of money who would marry you for the chance to become a count." She held up her hand. "Wives of earls are countesses, so the husband of an earl could be a count. Think about it. All you have to do is find someone who wants a title and marry him. Of course, he'd have to have piles of money, but you're an earl. Meeting people with money shouldn't be a problem."

He knew his mother was falling in love with the idea. The only problem was that she wasn't the one who was going to have to marry someone for money. Granted, he hadn't had much luck in the love-life department, but still he wasn't particularly interested in selling himself so he could fix up some family estate he hadn't known existed until a few days ago.

"Mum. That's crazy."

"No, it's not. I'm not saying you need to marry some prig you hate. But think about it. Earls and dukes have been doing this sort of thing for centuries. Who knows what you could get out of it? We got bloody Churchill from that kind of relationship. His mother was an American heiress." The more she warmed up to the idea, the more Robert wanted to crawl under the car and hide.

"That's enough. Like I said, I need to see what's in the estate and what my options are before I throw myself off the arranged marriage cliff."

"Who says it's an arranged marriage? There are dating sites and things like that on the Internet. We'll simply find you a gay matchmaker or something, like that show on American television." Her excitement made him more uncomfortable by the second. Where had this idea come from and how did he get it out of her head? "You go ahead and look into the estate. I'm going to go look into some things on my end."

"Mum. Just stop this whole thing right now. I'll come up with a plan to try to figure out what I'm going to do after my trip to the States. I don't need your help getting myself married off to some rich guy for his money. That isn't the kind of life that I want. None of this is."

He could see how his entire way of life was about to change. Up until then it had been the law firm and trying to help people who couldn't help themselves. And now he was supposed to be the Earl of Hantford and all that entailed, including looking after a huge pile of a house because it had been in his family… the family that had disowned his mother. This whole thing rubbed him the wrong way, and all he wanted was a way out of this mess. Selling everything seemed like that way to go. He could be rid of it and that would be that. Pay the taxes, put the rest in trust for the next generation, wherever that would come from, and say to hell with it all.

One look at his mother's set jaw and the gleam in her eyes told him that wasn't going to happen. Not even close. Lord help him—he was going to need it.

SCAN THE QR CODE BELOW TO PREORDER!

ANDREW GREY is the author of more than two hundred works of Contemporary Gay Romantic fiction, including an Amazon Editors Best Romance of 2023. After twenty-seven years in corporate America, he has now settled down in Central Pennsylvania with his husband of more than twenty-five years, Dominic, and his laptop. An interesting ménage. Andrew grew up in western Michigan with a father who loved to tell stories and a mother who loved to read them. Since then he has lived throughout the country and traveled throughout the world. He is a recipient of the RWA Centennial Award, has a master's degree from the University of Wisconsin–Milwaukee, and now writes full-time. Andrew's hobbies include collecting antiques, gardening, and leaving his dirty dishes anywhere but in the sink (particularly when writing). He considers himself blessed with an accepting family, fantastic friends, and the world's most supportive and loving partner. Andrew currently lives in beautiful, historic Carlisle, Pennsylvania.

Email: andrewgrey@comcast.net

Website: www.andrewgreybooks.com

HUNKS
OF THE
MONTH

ANDREW GREY

Former fashion photographer Sterling Vaughn reached the pinnacle of his profession only to have his life and heart come crashing down around him. Now he's attempting to rebuild his life as a portrait photographer in the town where he grew up.

Connor Hillyard is proud of his Scottish ancestry and dresses accordingly. The civic-minded college history professor has spent more of his life collecting degrees than experience. His only family is his sometimes matchmaking great-aunt Lucille, who thinks nothing of pulling him into her community gardening projects.

When Lucille needs a photographer for a calendar project to save her failing garden club, she recruits Sterling, who ropes Connor in as a model. Their eye-opening hunky gay calendar pulls the two men closer together. But just as things get interesting between them, the calendar polarizes the town, threatening to pull Sterling back into the high-profile world of fashion and away from the man who brought his heart back to life.

SCAN THE QR CODE
BELOW TO PREORDER!

STEAL MY
Heart

ANDREW GREY

Hilliard Bauman's life and his law practice are in Ohio, so when he inherits a home in California, his first instinct is to sell. Then again, his law partner is also his ex-partner, so maybe starting over wouldn't be so bad. Either way, he needs someone to fix up the house first. That's where Brian Mayer comes in.

Brian Mayer will do whatever work he can get, whether that means dog walking or painting fences. But in a small town where everyone knows everything about everyone, finding jobs can be difficult—especially if you've been wrongly convicted of theft. When Hilliard hires him to fix up his great-aunt's place, it's a relief on Brian's strained bank account… but tests Brian's heart to its limits.

As Hilliard digs into Brian's case and the botched investigation of the original crime, things really start heating up—both between him and Brian and in what should've been a cold case. This time when cops try to lay the blame at Brian's feet, he has Hilliard in his corner. Can they solve the mystery, put Brian's past to rest, and find a new beginning together?

Scan the QR Code
Below to Preorder!

ANDREW GREY
LOVE
AT FIRST SWIPE

Darby Wright has fought for his independence ever since he lost his sight as a child. But even now that he has his own home and a good job, his overprotective mother doesn't believe he can handle himself. Darby's determined to prove her wrong, but there are some things—like finding his guide dog's potty accident—where an extra set of eyes would come in handy.

Enter See For Me, an app that connects blind clients with sighted volunteers. See For Me is designed for just this sort of emergency, and it's through this app that Darby meets Reynaldo. Lust at first voice turns to more when Darby and Reynaldo run into each other at a local sandwich shop, where Renaldo seems as nice in person as he was in app.

With Reynaldo, Darby can feel his world expanding. Reynaldo doesn't just support him but understands him and sees Darby as more than his disability. But will being with Reynaldo mean giving up Darby's hard-fought independence, or will it mean gaining something more than he ever dreamed?

SCAN THE QR CODE BELOW TO PREORDER!

DEDICATED TO YOU
ANDREW GREY

Dillon Fitzgerald is a famous singer. He's also exhausted. Too many shows in a too busy schedule have left too little time for him to write or relax. He feels like the music is being strangled out of him. Some time is just what the doctor ordered, so when his friend offers him a week on a cruise, Dillon gets right on board. All he has to do is grow a little beard and hope no one recognizes him.

Financial advisor Tio Smythe-Barrett has been friends with Dillon forever. When the latest in a long string of girlfriends turns out to be a cheater, Tio offers her spot on what would have been a romantic vacation to Dillon instead. After all, why wouldn't he want to spend a week with his best friend?

As Tio and Dillon share close quarters, the boundaries in their friendship shift like the ocean currents. Spending time with Tio has Dillon's creative muse singing, and he can no longer deny that his feelings for Tio go beyond friendship. His heart soars when Tio responds to his flirting—but is he willing to risk what they have for the chance at true love?

SCAN THE QR CODE
BELOW TO PREORDER!

ONLY THE BRIGHTEST STARS

ANDREW GREY

The problem with being an actor on top of the world is that you have a long way to fall.

Logan Steele is miserable. Hollywood life is dragging him down. Drugs, men, and booze are all too easy. Pulling himself out of his self-destructive spiral, not so much.

Brit Stimple does whatever he can to pay the bills. Right now that means editing porn. But Brit knows he has the talent to make it big, and he gets his break one night when Logan sees him perform on stage.

When Logan arranges for an opportunity for Brit to prove his talent, Brit's whole life turns around. Brit's talent shines brightly for all to see, and he brings joy and love to Logan's life and stability to his out-of-control lifestyle. Unfortunately, not everyone is happy for Logan, and as Brit's star rises, Logan's demons marshal forces to try to tear the new lovers apart.

SCAN THE QR CODE
BELOW TO PREORDER!